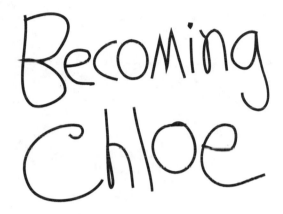

Becoming Chloe

CATHERINE RYAN HYDE

Alfred A. Knopf
New York

THIS IS A BORZOI BOOK PUBLISHED BY ALFRED A. KNOPF

Copyright © 2006 by Catherine Ryan Hyde

All rights reserved under International and Pan-American Copyright Conventions. Published in the United States by Alfred A. Knopf, an imprint of Random House Children's Books, a division of Random House, Inc., New York, and simultaneously in Canada by Random House of Canada Limited, Toronto. Distributed by Random House, Inc., New York.

KNOPF, BORZOI BOOKS, and the colophon are registered trademarks of Random House, Inc.

www.randomhouse.com/teens

Library of Congress Cataloging-in-Publication Data
Hyde, Catherine Ryan.
Becoming Chloe / Catherine Ryan Hyde.—1st ed.
    p.   cm.
SUMMARY: A gay teenage boy and a fragile teenage girl meet while living on the streets of New York City and eventually decide to take a road trip across America to discover whether or not the world is a beautiful place.
ISBN 0-375-83258-0 (trade) — ISBN 0-375-93258-5 (lib. bdg.)
[1. Homeless persons—Fiction. 2. Voyages and travel—Fiction.] I. Title.
PZ7.H96759Bec 2006
[Fic]—dc22
2005018949

Printed in the United States of America
March 2006
10 9 8 7 6 5 4 3 2 1
First Edition

For D., because hearts can do no more

ACKNOWLEDGMENTS

Many thanks to Laura Rennert (a.k.a. Agent Extraordinaire) and Michelle Frey (a.k.a. Editor I Dreamed I'd Get When I Was Young and Not At All Jaded) for sharing my vision for Jordy and Chloe. Thanks also to the trusted readers whose feedback helped shape the work: Anne Lowenkopf, Jim Surges, Analia Lovato, and Jane Patmore. Finally, special thanks to Dorothy Buhrman for loving Jordy so sincerely, and for handing me the perfect title when I was too close to the work to see it myself.

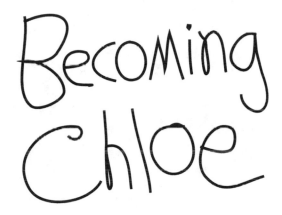

ONE

WINGS

The cellar has five high windows that let out onto the alley between this building and the next. I'm trying to get some sleep, only there are people having sex out there. I can hear the guy grunting the way guys do. Some guys. Not all guys. I never made a sound like that.

The girl is on her back on the hard concrete of that filthy alley, and I entertain the thought that maybe this was never her idea. That this is not a voluntary gig on her part. Because who gets turned on by lying in filth on cold concrete to do it? Then again, in this city, who knows? I've been in this city five days. Slept in this cellar three. Already I've seen people sink pretty low and not think twice about it. Lower than they probably thought they'd ever go. Too bad I'm one of them.

There's a streetlight out on the avenue, but not much light makes it down to the back of the alley. And even less makes it down here where I sleep. But at the street end of the alley there's a little bit of light, and I look down that way, and I see about three more pairs of feet.

I hear a guy say, "Someone's coming." He's talking in that kind of hoarse whisper they call a stage whisper, but this is definitely not the stage. This is so real it's starting to change me. Then he says, "No. Never mind. It's okay."

By now my stomach is all cold and I realize this is rape going on up there. I realize that my inconvenience at being kept awake doesn't stack up to much. I can think of at least one person in this direct vicinity who's having a much worse night than I am.

And I know I have to do something. I'm just not sure what.

I have to find a place to hide. Because I think I'm going to have to yell, and I don't want anyone to know where I'm yelling from. When I interrupt them, they're not going to like that. And the last thing I want is for them to come take out their frustrations on me. There's one cellar window that doesn't lock. If there wasn't, I wouldn't be down here. I jump up from the mattress too fast, and it makes me dizzy and makes my head hurt. My head still hurts a lot. I try not to think about it, but it's still pretty bad.

There's a kind of alcove created by mattresses stacked against the far wall. I hide behind those mattresses. And I try to decide what to do with my voice. Should I make it high, trying to pass for a woman? Or go deep, like a much bigger, much older guy than I am? Or just be me? I guess I'm looking to put on some authority.

I go deep. "I called the police!" I yell. Praying they can't track the direction of the sound. "I can see what's going on out there. I already called the police."

For a moment the whole world goes quiet and still. I can almost hear my heart pounding.

I peek around the mattresses. I still can't see the back of the alley very well in the dark, but I can see well enough to know that the scene of the actual rape is motionless. Just a lump of two figures frozen. And I can see the feet at the end of the alley and they're not moving, either.

I realize I've probably done all it's in my power to do, and it might not be nearly enough.

Then something miraculous happens. Actually, I don't guess it's fair to call it a miracle when it happens dozens of times a night. I listen to sirens all night here. Fire trucks, ambulances, police cars. Always an emergency close by. Back-to-back disasters, all night long. But the timing of this one is something like heaven. Or at least mercy.

The guys run away. All of them. And I come out of hiding.

I watch to see if the girl is going to be okay. She takes a minute getting up. One of her shoes is knocked off, and she looks around for it. Her jeans are only on one ankle but she worries about the shoe first. She moves off toward the end of the alley looking for it, and I can see her as she bends down to retrieve it. She's no older than I am. She's tiny. I wonder if I should go out there and see if she's okay.

Before I can even move she comes in through the window that doesn't lock. Drops right down into the cellar with me. Like she knew which one to go through all the time. Her jeans are still off except for that one leg, and her panties got ripped off, or she never had any, so she's more or less naked from the waist down, just standing there in a hooded sweatshirt, staring at me. She doesn't seem the least bit surprised that I'm here. She's blond,

3

with that long, perfectly straight hair that girls used to kill for in the sixties. Or so I've been told. A little younger than me, I think. She looks about sixteen but she's small for her age, or younger than I think. Pretty, with good bones in her face. Like she belongs someplace better than this. Then again, who doesn't?

"Hi," she says. She steps back into the other leg of her jeans and pulls them into place.

"You okay?" I ask.

"Oh. Me? Yeah. Sure. Sure. I'm fine."

She says it in a kind of distracted tone, like she has to keep reminding herself what we're talking about. I'm thinking maybe she's loaded, but her motor skills seem fine. She's putting her shoe back on now, a dirty white sneaker with the laces knotted and broken away.

"You sure?"

"Yeah. Sure. Fine."

"Want me to walk you home?"

"Home? I'm home now. I live *here*."

"No, you don't."

"Do too."

"I've been here for three nights. I'd have known it. I'd have seen you."

"I saw *you*," she says. She points to the little alcove behind the mattresses. "I saw you from there. I liked you. I already knew you were nice."

I spend about fifteen minutes trying to convince her that she should go to the hospital. Or the clinic. "They have to take you," I tell her, "even if you don't have money."

But she doesn't understand why she needs to see a doctor.

4

She doesn't understand what the doctor would do. Actually, I'm beginning to see there's a whole lot she doesn't understand.

"At least you should go to the health department. Make sure you didn't catch anything."

"What can you catch?" she wants to know.

"Like herpes or syphilis or AIDS."

"I never caught those before," she says. "Guys do that all the time. At the state home it was, like, almost every day. I never caught anything."

"Did you ever say no or try to fight?"

"It doesn't matter what you say. They don't ask. I never caught anything."

"You could have something and not know it. If you got a disease they could give you something for it."

"Well. Maybe in the morning," she says.

I can understand that she doesn't want to go out into the night again.

I still don't believe she's been living here. Not completely. But then I have to believe it, because she goes off into her little alcove and comes back with two blankets. I haven't had blankets since the money ran out. I've been looking for work but I'm not eighteen and nothing so far. I'm wishing I had a blanket. Maybe she'll loan me one. Maybe she'll be grateful to me. Right now she doesn't seem to know I did anything to help her. Right now she doesn't seem to know that she needed help. That something bad just happened.

Maybe in the morning she'll know more.

I lie down on my mattress. A moment later she lies down next to me, right up behind me, and throws both blankets over both of us. I don't say anything for a long time.

Finally I say, "I'm not going to try to do anything to you."

But I don't know why I bother to say that, because she obviously feels safe enough. I'm thinking that for three nights there was somebody here while I slept and I didn't even know it. She's feeling safer than I am.

"I know," she says.

"I don't even like girls."

"You don't like me?"

"I didn't mean that. I mean I don't like girls for sex."

"Who do you like for sex?"

"There's only two kinds of people. Girls and boys."

"I know."

"Let's not talk tonight," I say.

I still haven't figured out if she's crazy, or completely stupid, or stoned out of her mind. I'm not sure I even want to know. I just want to sleep, but I know I won't, because I'm still scared from what happened, and because there's a stranger in bed with me, and because something about her definitely isn't right.

In the morning we take the bus down to the health department. I could have had breakfast if I hadn't needed that bus fare. Now I haven't eaten or slept. But it's awful when you need a doctor and there's nobody with you and nobody cares. Believe me, I know.

I sit looking out the bus window and I realize I still don't know her name, so I ask.

"Wanda Johnston," she says.

"Oh."

"You don't like that name."

"I didn't say that."

"I could tell, though. I don't like it, either, but I'm stuck with it now. What can I do?"

"You can change your name."

"I can?"

"Sure. People will call you whatever you say they should."

"What should they call me? What's a good name?"

I think about that for a while. While I'm thinking, the city blocks roll past the window.

We pass by a public grade school and she says, "I used to go to school there. Before I went to the state home."

"Yeah? How old were you? Why did you have to go to a state home?"

"I don't know," she says. "Did you think of a good name yet?"

I cross "stoned" off the list of possibilities, because it doesn't seem to be wearing off.

"Maybe Kate or Jessica or Julie or Chloe."

"Chloe," she says. "Is that really a name?"

"Sure."

"How do you spell it?"

"C-h-l-o-e."

"You can't hear the 'h.' "

"No, but it's in there."

"Wow. A whole letter that it doesn't even have to use. That makes it pretty fancy."

The morning sun is coming through the bus window and lighting up her face. She has this cute, short nose, like a cheerleader. She actually looks like she could have been a cheerleader. She looks like she could have been the popular girl. Like she'd open her mouth and say something to make it sound like the world should revolve around her because she's pretty. But

7

instead she keeps talking like she doesn't even know there's a world around her. Like she doesn't know what world she's in.

She's looking at my forehead, and it makes her look sad. "Who hurt you?" she asks.

"It doesn't matter."

"Sure it does," she says. "It really does."

She goes in for the pelvic exam alone. After a while she comes out and sits with me again. Her shoulders seem tight, but maybe it's my imagination.

"Did it go okay?" I say. "Can we go?"

"They have to do HIV. We have to wait. How do they do HIV?"

"They have to draw some blood."

"How?"

"They just draw some out with a needle."

She jumps up and runs out of the waiting room, down the hall, and out onto the street. I run after her, but she's fast. I don't catch up until she hits the corner and has to yield to traffic.

"Hey, it's gonna be okay," I say. "Come back in."

"Not if there's needles."

"It won't hurt much. I'll go in with you. You can close your eyes. You'll never know."

I have my arm around her, and I'm leading her back in the direction of the health department. Her body feels stiff, but she isn't literally fighting me. I don't know her well enough to force her to do anything, but she seems like somebody who could get into a lot of trouble unless somebody cared enough to try. We go back inside and sit down again in the waiting room.

"You promise I won't even know?" Her eyes look glassy, like a wild animal about to be spooked into flight.

"I'll stay right with you. It hardly hurts."

When they call her number, a big black man in medical whites leads us into a small room and sits her down on an examining table.

"You can wait outside," he says.

"No, I can't," I say. "I promised her I'd come in. She's terrified of needles."

"Great," he says. "Let's just get this over with."

He ties off her arm with a rubber tube, rubs and pats at a vein until he likes what he sees. Then he turns around and breaks the cap off a sterile needle and she screams and rolls off the table. Lands in a ball between the table and the wall, yelling.

The big guy looks exasperated. "The point of this is not to draw blood against her will," he says. "There has to be some voluntary cooperation involved."

"Look, she got raped last night and she's scared of needles. Can you cut her some slack?"

"Can you get her back on the table?"

I have to literally lift her and put her back on the table. She's still curled up in a ball, and her arm is still tied off.

"I'm going to hold you," I tell her. "I'm not holding you like forcing you. I'm just holding real tight so you don't get scared, okay?"

I pin her body down with the weight of my own. I also put one hand over her eyes because I promised her she wouldn't have to see. The guy manages to get the tied-off arm out from underneath her, and he quickly and expertly slides the needle home. Blood jumps into the tube. Then her head moves sideways, away from my hand, and she opens her eyes and screams. She tries to jump off the table but I hold her down hard because I'm scared she'll break off the needle in her arm or something.

"Could you hurry?" I say to the guy, because I know I can't hold her for long. She's in this adrenaline-fueled state that's very hard to overpower.

Before I can even finish the sentence she sinks her teeth into my arm. The fleshy part of my left arm just below the elbow. She locks on like a pit bull and just keeps sinking in. I yell out loud, and I let go, but she doesn't.

The guy pulls the needle free, and I'm screaming, and she's really in deep now. I have a sick, horrible sense that she's about to hit bone. She has this jaw that just won't quit and the pain is incredible and I don't know how to make her let go. I think maybe I'll have to slap her, but I just can't bring myself to do it. The clinic guy holds up the needle so she can see that he's done and way over on the other side of the room with it. He holds up both hands, like a surrender, and she opens her jaws and lets me go. A stream of blood runs down my arm and I sit down hard on the floor and wonder why she didn't have all that fight last night in the alley. Why I had to be the one to bring that out in her.

She rolls off the table again and balls up by the wall, shivering.

The clinic guy looks closely at my arm and whistles. "You'll have to get that looked at. I wish I could help you here, but we're only equipped for these certain types of medicine."

"Right." I'm surprised I say anything at all. I think I might be in a little bit of shock.

"You should have that head wound looked at, too. How old are those stitches?"

"Nine days, I think. Or ten." I'm not sure how long I was in the hospital. That time is mostly a blur.

"It's not healing very well. It looks infected. It looks like you didn't keep it clean enough. I wouldn't take chances with a head wound like that one."

"Right," I say. And think how badly I want to go home. I wish I had one.

"You're not getting out of here without a tetanus shot," he says.

So I sit up on the table and he gives me a tetanus shot. I look down at the little pit bull and she's sitting up now, pretty calm, watching me.

"You're much better at that than I am," she says.

I'll be damned if I'm spending my pitiful lunch money on getting us home. Especially her. I'm going to need to eat something. So I set off walking, even though it's three or four miles.

I keep looking over my shoulder and she keeps being back there. Following me.

"I'm really sorry I bit you," she says.

"Me, too."

"I don't even know your name."

"Jordan."

"I'm really sorry I bit you, Jordan."

"Leave me alone," I say. "Stop following me."

I'm crossing against traffic, walking right out in front of cabs and making them stop for me. Because I'm pissed. My arm is throbbing, with this intense shot of pain on every throb like somebody's hammering a sharp wedge of metal into it with a big sledgehammer. I'm trying to think if my head even hurt this much.

"But we live in the same place," she says.

"I'll find a new place."

I'll get a job. And maybe some painkillers, or antibiotics, or both. I'll be able to afford food every day. This is just a bad week in my life. I'm not going to have to live like this much longer.

I stop at a phone booth and call information to find a free clinic. It's not that far from the cellar where I've been sleeping.

She stands and waits while I'm on the phone, then follows me again as I walk away.

"Go away, Wanda," I yell over my shoulder.

"My name is Chloe," she says.

"Go away, Chloe."

But she follows me all the way to the free clinic. Where the woman at the counter tells me that to see an actual doctor I would have to come back at six-thirty p.m. Six-thirty to midnight.

"What kind of clinic is open from six-thirty to midnight?" I ask.

"The kind that treats overdoses and stab wounds," she says.

Meanwhile this Chloe/Wanda person is still following me. Still standing behind me.

"I'll go in with you," she says. "You won't even feel anything."

I'm lying on the mattress and Chloe is sitting by my side, stroking my hair.

"Want me to go see what time it is?" she asks for the fiftieth time. Every hour or so she's been jogging down to the corner drugstore to check the clock.

"Not yet," I say.

"I used to have a bird that bit me all the time. But I still loved him."

"It was a dumb animal," I say. "It didn't know any better."

"I still loved him," she says. "Didn't you ever have a pet that bit you?"

"I never even had a pet."

"Why not?"

"My mother doesn't like animals."

"That's really sad. Want me to go see what time it is again?"

"Yeah. Good idea." Anything to get rid of her. "What happened to your bird?" I ask before she climbs out the window.

"I don't know. I had to go to the state home. He didn't get to go."

"What was his name?"

"Malcolm."

"Malcolm? Why did you name your bird Malcolm?"

"I don't know," she says. And disappears.

Only she doesn't come back in a minute or two with the time. She doesn't come back, period. Which I'm thinking is just as well.

My arm hurts like hell and my head hurts a lot more than it did yesterday and I feel like I might have a fever. I try to sleep but I keep dreaming I'm in pain and it wakes me up. The last time I wake up it's dark already. So it's way past six-thirty.

I walk down to the free clinic but there's a line down the block. I stand in it for a minute or two, too dizzy to stand much longer. I'm thinking of sitting right down on the cold pavement. But then a guy in his forties comes down the line and says the doctor is really swamped and if you're not bleeding to death could you please come back tomorrow.

So I sigh, and I walk home. Stop at the all-night restaurant like I always do, to use the restroom. Wash up as best I can. My arm is swollen now, with black and purple around the bite marks. It helps not to try to move it at all.

When I get in, I hear a slight rustling noise. It's coming from behind the mattress alcove.

"Chloe?" I say.

"No," she says, shyly, like she knows she isn't wanted. "Did you get your doctor?"

"No."

"Oh. I'm sorry." She comes out and sits on my mattress with me. She has something in the front pouch pocket of her hooded sweatshirt. "I have a present for you," she says.

She sounds so serious and intense—scared that I won't like it—that I get scared, too.

"What is it?" My voice comes out gentle. I wonder why I don't get to be mad anymore.

She slips it out from her big front pocket and sets it on the mattress with me. It's a pigeon. A live pigeon. It just sits there, blinking. "How did you catch it?"

"I don't know," she says. "He just let me."

"I think it might have a broken wing." I can see one of its wings hanging down too far.

"Maybe. I got him for you because you never had a pet. Do you like him?"

I reach out to the bird and he lets me stroke his back. I don't

14

know if he's tame, or just in shock, or too sick or wounded to re-act, but he lets me touch him. "Yeah," I say. "I like him."

"Would you like him if he bit you?"

"I don't know. Does he bite hard?"

"He doesn't bite at all," she says. "I just wondered."

I sleep for what feels like a long time, but when I wake up it's still dark. And I feel sick. I feel like I have a bad fever. I need to pee. I touch my forehead and it hurts more than it should. It's puffy. The stitches feel like they're about to pull right out, they're so tight.

Chloe is sitting in a corner, in the one little bit of light from the avenue street lamp. She's breaking pieces off a hot-dog bun and feeding them to the pigeon. "You slept a long time," she says. "It's later tonight than it was yesterday night when you went to sleep."

"Are you sure I slept a whole day?"

"Positive. I tried to wake you up before the line at the clinic got real long again. But I couldn't wake you up. And it's long."

"Where did you get a hot dog?"

"I don't have a hot dog," she says. She holds it out for me to see. Just an empty bun, with a smear of mustard. "The hot dog was already gone when I found it. Here, I brought you this cup," she says. She moves over to hand me an empty Styrofoam coffee cup with a lid. The bird skitters out of her way into the darkness. "You can pee in this, and then I'll take it outside and throw it away."

"That was smart." That seems too smart for her. "That was smart to figure out that I'd need a way to pee."

"No, it wasn't," she says.

✳ ✳ ✳

When I wake up again it's light. Chloe is leaning over me. She has the bird tightly up against her belly, and when she sees my eyes come open, she puts him down on my chest, and I hold him and stroke his back. I notice that she has a nasty bruise inside her elbow where the blood was drawn, because we never got pressure on it like you're supposed to.

"You popped a couple of stitches," she says. "It looks disgusting. Here. I brought you some soup." She hands me an open paper cup. It's chicken noodle. It's still warm.

"Where did you get soup?"

"I told the guy down at the deli that my friend Jordy was really really sick and you needed something to eat. So you really like him, huh?" She points with her chin to the bird.

"Yeah," I say. "I really do. Thanks for the soup."

While I'm drinking it, I think how I have to get to the clinic tonight. Even if I have to crawl.

"I would like you even if you hurt me," she says.

"But that's just it. I would never hurt you."

She starts to cry. And then I feel like shit because I made her cry. She has these eyes that are blue and green and gray all at the same time, and they're huge. When she cries they get even bigger, like those corny-sad paintings of kids or clowns.

"Well, I wish you would. Because then I could forgive you, and then you'd see."

"I'm sorry," I say. "I'm really sorry I made you cry."

"That's okay," she says, brightening some. "I like you anyway."

I wake up and it's dark again, and the fever is making me feel like I don't exist. Somewhere in the back of my brain I'm thinking, Oh, shit, I'm still not getting to the clinic. But it's a weird thought. Weird and far away. Chloe is gone, but I can see the bird walking around in the spill of light from the avenue street lamp. And I think I might die here. Because I can't get anywhere now, like this, and I'm not going to get any better. I'm so sick that I almost don't mind the thought of dying, but I really mind doing it here.

What seems like an hour later—but it could be a minute or a day—Chloe drops back in through the window. She has a Styrofoam cup in her hand and her pockets are stuffed.

"Here," she says. She holds out a capsule on the palm of her hand. "Take this."

"What is it?"

"Antibiotic."

"Where did you get it?"

"Will you just take it? Here, here's some water."

"That's not the cup I've been peeing in, is it?"

"Of course not. It's fresh. Here. Take two aspirin, too. To help get the fever down."

"How did you get them to give you all this?"

"Just shut up and take them."

I swallow all three pills at once.

Then Chloe takes a tube of ointment out of her sweatshirt pocket and squeezes some onto my forehead and some onto both sides of my arm. I jump when she touches each of those places. Last of all, she unwraps a butterfly bandage and uses it to reseal the split on my forehead. I shout out loud because it hurts.

"How did you get them to give you all that, Chloe?"

"I just told them what was wrong with you. I told them I'd never get you down there unless we could do something about the fever. Oh. Here." She goes back into her pocket and takes out a scrap of paper. "This is the number of the doctor. *Where he lives*," she says, with great awe. "If you call him when you're okay enough to go down there, he'll meet you on his lunch hour. He wants to make sure you're okay."

I stare at the number for a minute, then drink the rest of the water. I'm so thirsty I could die right now, just from that. "That took a lot of brains, Chloe. To get all this done."

"No, it didn't," she says.

The bird flies unsteadily into one of the windows and then flaps down to the floor again.

It's five or six days before I get in to see the doctor. But I'm feeling much better.

I'm feeling clean because I took a sponge bath in a public restroom. Chloe let me use her towel. Who knew she had a towel? She has a lot of stuff in that alcove that I haven't seen yet.

The doctor has gray hair but looks too young to have it. He looks like a guy who really cares but now he's worn out from it. He's small and mostly refined-looking, except for a full beard. He's attractive. I feel attracted to him the minute he walks into the room. Then I see a wedding ring on his finger and I feel ashamed. And I try to feel something else entirely.

"The famous Jordan," he says.

It embarrasses me. "I'm not famous."

"You are around here."

He peels off the butterfly bandage and I try to not yell out. I don't want to be a coward in front of him. I want to be brave.

"Your girlfriend really loves you," he says.

"She's not my girlfriend. Are you going to have to stitch that again?"

"No, it's starting to heal. I'm just going to take out the old ones. It'll hurt. I'm sorry." He's right. It hurts like hell. But I don't make any noise. "Your sister?" he asks.

"No, she's just a friend."

"Damn good one," he says. "She waited in line all night, and when we tried to lock up she sat down cross-legged on the floor and wouldn't leave. We had to give her antibiotics and aspirin just to get her out the door."

"Did she seem . . ." Then I don't know how to finish that thought.

"What?"

"I'm not sure how to say it. Did she seem . . . smart?"

He thinks a minute. Shrugs. "Smart enough, I guess. Why?"

"I'm just having trouble figuring her out. Sometimes she's . . . Well, like when I met her, she'd just been raped. And she wasn't even upset about it. She just said it happened all the time. I asked her if she ever said no, and she said it doesn't matter what she says. It's like she doesn't even understand what a bad thing is. She doesn't even know that what's happening to her isn't okay. Then when she needs to get something done, she seems a lot smarter."

He has his hand on my shoulder now, but I wish he wouldn't. Because it makes me think things that I feel ashamed about. And because I think he'll see that I'm attracted to him. Like he'll all of a sudden know me way too well.

"Maybe she doesn't want to understand things that she doesn't think she can change anyway. Maybe sometimes you just have a couple of rotten choices. Like you can fail to comprehend the world you've got, or you can see it as this ugly, evil, dangerous place and not be able to do a damn thing about it."

"So you think it's an emotional thing?"

"I don't know. I don't know enough about her. I just know the kinds of things I've seen over the years." I look at his face and I see what he means. About the things he's seen over the years. He's seen too much. "I wouldn't rule out severe trauma. Of course, it's just a theory. But don't rule it out. And don't underestimate it."

"So if that's it, could she get better? I mean, if somebody made her feel safe and took care of her? Could she get better?"

"I don't know how to answer that question. I can't predict the future. I think a better question would be, Does she have anybody in her life who cares enough to do all that for her?"

He still has his hand on my shoulder, but now it doesn't matter because I'm thinking about Chloe. "I'm not sure," I say. "I guess I'd have to think about that."

"Do you *know* the person who did this to your head, Jordan?"

I look down at the clinic floor, which is linoleum. Very old linoleum. I wonder what he'll do if I don't answer.

When he gets tired of waiting he says, "Okay, let me put it another way. Is this someone you still have to see on a regular basis?"

"No, sir."

"Good. That's mostly what I needed to know."

On the way home I stop at Chloe's old grade school. Okay, I'm lying. It's not on the way home. It's eleven blocks out of my way.

But I go there all the same. Because I just have to know about all this. I go into the office and a woman asks if she can help me. She's about fifty, with a round face. She seems nice, which makes me uneasy. Then I realize the doctor was nice, too.

This is my problem. I'm not used to people being nice to me. Not lately, anyway. I'm not sure how to deal with that.

"Did Wanda Johnston used to go to school here?"

The woman looks her up on the computer. "You realize I can't give out any of this information unless you're family. I can't show you her records."

"I just want to know what she can do," I say. "I want to know how bad it is."

"How bad what is?"

"I mean, was she in, like, a special ed class? I'm only asking because I want to help her. Somebody has to. Help her."

She sighs.

I say, "Look. If anybody else was trying to help her . . . If anybody else had ever tried to help her . . . ." Then I give her a look that I hope is like the one Chloe gives me when she wants me to forgive her. All kind of big-eyed and sad. Because I know that's a hard one to resist. "Maybe you could just tell me what it can't do any harm to tell me?"

She sighs again and pulls up Chloe's files from the computer. "No special ed. Just the regular class, with everybody else. Look. What I'm supposed to tell you is exactly nothing. I'm not allowed to tell you that she was here for first and second grade and part of third. And that her grades were normal. And then she was turned over to Child Protective Services. So you don't know that. Because I didn't tell you."

"Can you also not tell me why?"

"That I don't know. We're talking about a *big* loop of secrecy now. And I'm not in it."

She's turned the monitor screen just a little bit toward me, which is how I happen to find out that Chloe was eighteen on the twelfth of May.

I don't see Chloe once all day. I have no idea where she goes. All I see is the bird, fluttering around the cellar, apparently feeling like himself again. All dressed up with nowhere to go. I wonder how hard it will be to convince Chloe that we need to turn him loose.

Then I think maybe she's gone, out of my life for good, and it doesn't even matter. I can't decide if that's what I want or not.

I come back from the all-night restroom around midnight, and she's back. I don't ask from where.

"Careful," she says as I come in through the window. "Don't let the bird out."

We sit and watch him fly in endless circles around the room. It occurs to me that I never bothered to name him, but it seems like bad timing to do it now.

"Wow, he's feeling good, huh?" I say.

"Yeah, but he doesn't like for me to touch him now."

"Well, he's probably feeling more like a bird these days."

"Want to go get something to eat? I have money."

"Where did you get money?"

"Some old guy in the park said he felt sorry for me because I'm too skinny, and he gave me five dollars."

"Great," I say. "Because I'm starving."

* * *

We eat hot dogs and fries, and while we're eating I feel so much better that I almost feel happy. Happy. This weird thing I've forgotten how to feel.

"That doctor was really nice," I say.

"Yeah. I liked him okay. Did he say you were going to be okay?"

"Yeah. He thinks probably I'll be okay." And just for a minute I guess I do, too. The doctor and the food, and being clean, and having met people who were pretty nice to me, all in one day.

"Wow," she says. "You're really feeling better."

"Yeah," I say. "I guess I am."

When we get home we lie down and try to sleep, but the bird is making such a racket. He's flapping around in the dark, bouncing off the mattresses and banging into the windows. I feel bad for him. I feel bad for me because I figure this will go on all night and I'm tired.

Chloe says, "Jordy. Are you asleep?"

"How can I sleep with all that racket going on?"

"I have to talk to you about something. I know this is going to be hard for you to hear. Because he's your first pet and all. But I really think we're going to have to let the bird go now."

It takes a long time to catch up with him, but I follow him around, and he's getting tired. Wearing down. Finally I manage to get him into a corner, and I pick him up with my hand firmly around his body, holding down his wings. It's extra hard because I can't really use my left hand much. I can't even move those

23

fingers right now because it pulls into the muscles in my arm and hurts like hell. But I try not to make a big thing of that around Chloe. She feels bad enough as it is. When I get the bird, I put him up under my shirt and then tuck it in again. I think he'll run around and scratch me, but something about that dark, confined space calms him. He holds still.

We climb up out of the cellar window, which, believe me, isn't easy. Not with a pigeon in your shirt and only one working hand. But then I make it and we're out into the night, which feels cool and open. It feels like being free.

I can feel the bird against my belly. Feel his soft feathers. He has his little talons wrapped around the waistband of my jeans. For some reason this makes me feel close to him. Like he really is my pet now. Like we finally fit together, just as we're about to come apart.

We cross the street and Chloe says, "Not here."

"Okay," I say, though I don't know why. Ten blocks later I ask, "Where are we going?"

"The park."

In a way it makes sense. In another way it doesn't.

"But if we let him off here . . . wouldn't he pretty much fly to the park anyway?"

"Maybe," she says. "But he might bump into a building on the way. He's just sort of still getting his wings back."

We stand together in the park and I look around and breathe more consciously than usual.

"Do you feel bad?" Chloe asks.

"No. I feel good. Why?"

"Well. He's your pet."

"But it's not like something bad was happening to him. This is a good thing for him."

"And it's not like he's not going to be yours. He's just going to be yours out there instead of in the cellar. You might not see him anymore, but wherever he is, he's still yours."

"I agree," I say.

I take him out from under my shirt. He looks around at the night much the way I've been doing. I turn him around, open my hands. He doesn't move.

He just sits there on my two open hands, facing out into the world.

Then he unfolds those wings but he still doesn't fly away. It's almost like he's trying to believe he really can. The right wing still looks a little on the droopy side. Maybe it always will. Maybe he'll never be exactly as good as new again, but at least he can fly with it. That seems like the main thing. His wingspan looks so big to me, across my open hands. A foot, maybe. Or nearly. Big, capable, only slightly damaged wings.

I feel him push against my hands as he lifts away. I can feel the downdraft of his wings, the pressure of the evening air against my palms. He flaps almost horizontally toward a tree, gaining only a little bit of altitude. He sits on the branch for a while.

"Maybe he feels bad leaving you."

"Maybe he's tired from running into the cellar windows all day."

I turn my head to look at a man with a big yellow dog, and when I turn back, my first and only bird has flown away.

On the way back to the cellar, Chloe says, "Thanks for the new name. It's like that other person whose name I'm not even saying is just gone."

"Don't you want another one?"

"No. Chloe is good."

"I don't mean instead of Chloe. I mean a last name."

"No. I don't even need one. Chloe is such a good name I don't even need another one."

I find it touching, almost enviable, that a person with so little feels she has all she needs.

TWO

THE CELLAR KING

Chloe says, "Wow. Raymond lives here?"

"Yeah, Chlo. Right up there."

We're standing with our backs to Central Park, looking up at his building.

"Raymond is rich," she says.

"No," I say. "Not rich. Just regular."

"Who's richer?"

"Lots of people, Chlo."

"Do we know them?"

"No," I say. "No, we don't know them."

"Oh," she says. "Too bad."

Raymond comes to the door in that paisley silk smoking jacket and those skinny pale legs sticking out underneath. He's not a skinny guy, Raymond, not by a long shot. But he seems to have special places for holding fat, and his legs aren't one of them. He is a lovely man. Just not on the outside. Just not in a very attractive package.

"Jordan," he says. "Oh. I see you brought your friend." He looks from me to Chloe, who curtsies. Chloe is having one of her princess days.

"She won't be any trouble at all, Raymond, I promise." I take Chloe's hand and we sweep past him into his living room before he can say no. "Chloe is going to stay out of our way completely. Chloe is going to take a nice hot bubble bath fit for a princess and not come in the bedroom once the whole time." I shuffle her off into Raymond's big master bath. "Did you bring clean underwear?" I say this last quietly, for only her to hear. I start the water running.

"You didn't say to."

"Damn it, Chlo, I did say to. I told you to."

"Don't be mad at me, Jordy. Maybe I wasn't listening. I'm sorry."

Chloe stands in the middle of Raymond's big bathroom, looking all around and above her, the way people do in art museums and cathedrals. I should know. We spend a lot of time in art museums and cathedrals. Meanwhile, she's taking off her jeans. I help her by pulling her big red sweatshirt inside out over the top of her head.

"Take your panties off and put them to soak in the sink," I say, and then I go into Raymond's bedroom to get a pair of his Jockey shorts.

He's facing away from me, looking out the window, removing the smoking jacket. I like it better when he's all tucked under the covers when I get in. He glances over his shoulder, watches me take a pair of light-blue Jockeys out of his underwear drawer, but says nothing.

Chloe is naked, dipping her toe in the water, when I get back to her.

"Wait for the bubbles," I say.

I find the bubble bath under the sink and squirt about three baths' worth into her water. Bubbles roar up out of nowhere. Threaten to take over the world.

"Jordy? Do princesses ever take baths with no bubbles?"

"Oh, I doubt that. Put these on when you're done," I say, and hold up the Jockeys for her to see. I turn off the water, purposely leaving the bath a little low in case Chloe splashes

She reaches out and puts her hand through the fly opening. "Jordy, what would I use this for?"

"You won't. But they're clean. Now I want you to stay in here the whole time, and not come in the bedroom once. Not for any reason. And I want you to sing the whole time. That way I'll know where you are."

"What should I sing?"

"Anything you want. You pick something. Have a nice bubble bath, Chlo."

As I join Raymond in bed I hear her sing the first few lines of "A Whiter Shade of Pale."

We're naked under the covers together. "She has a lovely voice," Raymond says. This is the first I realize that we're both listening to Chloe's song. I can hear Chloe get to the end of that long song and start over again at the beginning. That same song again. Chloe never chooses two different things both on the same day. "I know she's your girlfriend, but it's okay."

"She's not, though, Raymond. It's not like that with us."

"Either way, it's okay."

Raymond doesn't believe I'm really gay, because of Chloe. I don't work too hard to convince him. If he knew I really was, then he'd know it really was just him. I mean, he's fifty-something to my seventeen, for Christ's sake. It's not Raymond's fault he's fifty. It's not my fault I can't feel much for him. We're all just running around being exactly what we are.

Then silence. No "A Whiter Shade of Pale." I wait two beats, three. I'm just about to jump out of bed when I hear the first couple of random chords on Raymond's big grand piano. Chloe has a flair for almost all creative things, like singing. But in this case she's curious about the piano. Not trying to make music so much as noise. Playing it the way a small dog would if you put him up there to tramp around on the keys.

"What's wrong with her?" Raymond asks. Then right away I know he can feel my body tighten up, and he pulls back to his own side of the bed a ways. "I'm sorry, I just meant—" Raymond is a little bit afraid of me. The way it should be.

"Nothing is wrong with her. Why would you say a thing like that?"

"I just meant . . . She just seems . . . childlike."

"So? What's wrong with that?"

"Nothing," he says. "Nothing at all."

I sit up on the edge of his bed and begin to dress. "I'll bring the underwear back. Clean."

"Don't bother," Raymond says. "It's okay. So. Listen. Are you doing okay this week? Financially, I mean. Are you having an okay week financially?"

"Well, not really, Raymond, no. Frankly, things are tight. Frankly, if you could help out a little, that would be great."

"You know I never mind helping out."

"You know you're never obligated."

"Yes, yes, of course," Raymond says.

We go through this same little dance every week. Just so we both know that we both know that all the rules are still in place. Just to keep making sure all those loose ends lie down exactly the way they're supposed to.

He gives me four clean twenties. "I hope this will help your situation," he says.

"Very much, Raymond. You're a dear to help out."

I kiss him on the lips and he sighs.

I'm pulling her down the street by her hand. We're walking fast, crossing against the lights. Stopping traffic. "What do you want to eat, Chlo?"

"Something good."

"Well, of course," I say. "We all want to eat something good. What I'm asking is, what kind of food do you think would be good right now?"

"Hmm," she says. "Hmm. Maybe strawberry waffles with whipped cream."

"It's four in the afternoon, Chlo."

"So? Don't they make them at four?"

"Maybe somewhere, but I don't know where. Most places make them at breakfast."

"I didn't get breakfast."

"I know," I say. "I'm sorry." It was Raymond day, and we were a little strapped.

"I think a princess always gets breakfast." When she says this she lets her hand slip out of mine and I lose her in a crowd.

I poke around and find her standing in front of a shop window, looking in. "Never let go of my hand on the street, Chlo, you know that." Hand-holding avoids two major problems. Chloe getting lost. Even lost for a minute is bad. One day I left her at the Chock full o'Nuts drinking coffee with six sugars while I saw Raymond; she was supposed to sit right there but it took us five hours to connect up again. I haven't figured out how to fix those big losts, so I work on holding her hand so she won't get lost for even a minute. And also, even though I don't look like someone who'd be straight, people figure I must be anyway, and I almost never get bashed anymore.

It's a leather store she's standing in front of. "Wow, Jordy, look at that leather coat."

I don't know yet that my life will turn out differently if I don't.

It's a duster coat, like mine. Only a million times nicer. Really long, almost full length, with a split up the back like those great Australian riding coats.

My own duster coat has seen better decades. It's a tweedy fabric, going a little threadbare, but still sharp in a battered sort of way. But the lining is starting to fall apart. Chloe sews it, all the time. I lifted a little sewing kit from the drugstore, and every time a piece of lining hangs down under the hem, she sews it. It's a thing that can't go on indefinitely.

Without my duster coat I'd be nothing.

The coat we're looking at is black leather, with slash pockets. Not even really shiny, more a matte black. When I look at it, I make that sound Raymond always wishes I could make with him. I remember what it feels like to want something. If I had that coat, I'd be magic. Men would cross the city to fall down at my feet. I'd turn the collar up, roll the sleeves back two turns, push them up a little toward my elbows. Everybody who saw me would want me, and I'd understand why. It would seem natural to be all that to someone. To everyone.

"We can't afford that coat," I say.

"You didn't even ask what it costs yet."

"Trust me on this," I say. The guy in the store—the clerk—is this young skinhead guy, and he's watching us like he has a gun under the counter and maybe it's time to get it.

"Hey, mister," Chloe calls out. "How much is that coat?"

"Five seventy-five," he says, comfortably smug in knowing this will make us go away.

We go away.

"You would look great in that coat, Jordy."

"Stop talking about it," I say. It hurts to talk about it. Like sitting around talking about what a great guy that was who just dumped you, how good-looking he was, and how great he was in bed. I've lost something I couldn't afford to lose. "What do you want to eat, Chlo? Have you decided yet?"

"Something good," she says.

While Chloe is eating the last of her curly fries, I tell her, "I have to run to the bank before it closes. And you have to wait right here. Right here. The whole time. I'm going to bring you back a present. If you don't wait right here, you don't get it, though."

"What happens to my present if I don't wait right here?"

"You don't get it."

"Where does it go, though? It doesn't just disappear."

"Back to the store," I say. "It goes right back to the store for a refund if you're not here when I get back."

I don't literally run to the bank, because I don't look dignified running. No one does. I look like a sneak thief when I run. I stride to the bank. I put two of Raymond's twenties in our savings account. Now we have $210 in the bank. So after dinner and Chloe's present—if I can find something cheap—we'll have maybe $30 to last the whole week. Or better yet, I'll hustle up some more. The more I stash in the bank, I figure the more likely I am to hustle up some more.

I stop at the drugstore and buy Chloe a pad of construction paper and a set of six colored markers. This I figure will keep her out of my hair for hours.

When I get back, some guy is sitting with Chloe, trying to pick her up. She's laughing that flirty little laugh and flipping her hair around with first one hand, then the other. That long blond hair. She's just about the whitest white girl who ever walked. She is eighteen years old and slim and blond and pretty and doesn't even know all the reasons why to say no. She might as well wear a sign on her back that says GET SOME HERE. She might as well walk down the street with a freaking bull's-eye painted on her ass.

I pull the guy out of the booth by his arm. Trouble is, he stands up to be a lot taller than me. But I don't care. He's about twice my age, plus he looks like he works out daily. But I don't care. "Goodbye," I say.

"You her boyfriend?"

"Goodbye."

We stand frozen while he decides. We don't break each other's gaze. Classic dogfight stance. Two mutts circling for territory, only one mutt is fighting for more. I'm fighting to protect a loved one. He just wants to get laid. Watch out for the mutt with more on the line.

He looks down at Chloe, like to decide if she's worth the hassle. Then he tugs at the collar of his jacket and I know it's over. "Yeah, whatever," he says as he walks away.

I sit down across from Chloe, who still hasn't finished her curly fries. They must be really cold by now.

"I don't know what you're mad about," she says. "I waited right here."

On the way back to the cellar we stop in that all-night restaurant and use their bathrooms. Last thing, always. Hopefully we won't have to tramp down there again in the middle of the night.

We put a new little lock on the window with the broken one. Every morning we climb out through it and leave it unlocked. Then we lock it after ourselves when we get in, so nobody else can get the bright idea to sleep down there. Someday we may show up and find out somebody else went in and locked it behind them, beating us out for the night. Trapping in all our stuff. Not that all our stuff is much. But it hasn't happened yet.

When we get in and locked up, I go through the nightly ritual. There are mattresses up against a wall. I take the outside one and let it down onto the floor. Then I get our box. It's in with a bunch of other boxes, where I can't imagine anybody is going to notice it by day. We leave it different places, under other things, in the middle of piles, so it won't attract attention. In it are our blankets. We have two, but maybe when winter sets in again for real we can get a third. Who knows? And then some things we don't use every day, like the sewing kit and the scissors Chloe uses to cut my hair. And her pictures, and the tape. I have to tape the pictures up on the wall beside the bed, every night, or she'll never get any sleep and so neither will I.

I kneel on the mattress and tape them up one by one. They're all houses. Cut or torn from newspapers and magazines. And they all have green lawns and bushes or trees.

Meanwhile, Chloe is like a cat in the dark. She can see in all kinds of blackness. She's sitting in the tiniest bit of light, a ray of it that washes through the street-side window, from the corner street lamp. She's drawing something with her markers.

"Shit," I say. "We just ran out of tape."

She looks up at me, sees I'm holding the very last of her house pictures. Number eleven, I think. A new one. I didn't even know she had this one. At least, I don't think I did. It's hard to see in this light. It's hard to keep track.

"Just set that last one up against the wall where I can see it."

"You know it's not going to look like this, right, Chlo? You do know there won't be trees or grass." Or a house for that matter. We'd be lucky to get a studio.

"You always say that to me, Jordy."

"I know. I just want to make sure you didn't forget."

"We can get more tape tomorrow, right?"

"This might be a tight week, Chlo." Like they're not all.

"You could lift some." She's gone back to her work now. She's taken up the scissors from our box and she's cutting the paper into some kind of intricate design.

36

"I don't know if it's worth going to jail for."

"They wouldn't put you in jail for just tape, would they?"

"Might. Never can tell. Depends on the mood people are in."

"Well, I have to have tape, or I can't finish this." But she looks finished. She's put the markers and the scissors away in our box.

"What are you making?"

"It's for you," she says. "It's a crown." She brings it over to me and holds it in place around my head. But it won't stay in one piece in the back. Not without tape. She has a point about that. "There you have it. King Jordy."

"What am I the king of?" I feel tired all of a sudden. Too tired to rule.

"Well. This. Where we live."

I laugh. "All this, huh?"

"Well, it's something. And at least you're the king of it."

"No, that's good, Chlo. You're right. It's good to be king of something. I bet you could figure out how to make it stay without tape."

I take it off and look. It's amazingly intricate, in five colors, with cutout paper filigree and a snake weaving in and out. How she does these things, I'll never know.

"It's beautiful, Chlo." She takes it from me and figures out how to cut a tab and slot with the scissors. I'm impressed. I say, "You know I can only wear it down here in the cellar, though. I can't wear it on the street." I figure she'll ask why not in a second, so I beat her to it. "Because I'm not the king of anything up there."

Chloe nods thoughtfully. "Right," she says. "That's exactly the point."

I set the crown on the corner of our mattress and we go to sleep the way we always do, blankets pulled up to our chins, Chloe draped over my back like she wants to get inside my skin but hasn't yet managed to get any closer than this.

In the morning I leave her at Chock full o'Nuts to drink coffee with six sugars. I give her two dollars in case the waitress starts thinking Chloe can't pay. It doesn't work to have things like that happening while I'm away.

"I have to go see Rene," I say. "So this could take a while. I could even be two hours. You have to wait here the whole time."

"Boring," she says.

"I know. I'm sorry." I see a newspaper over on the next table, an empty table with a newspaper someone up and left behind. "Here," I say, and get it for her, and set it on the table in front of her. "You can look for pictures."

"Get tape," she says.

"Yeah, okay. Don't go away this time."

"Lift it if you have to."

I give her that look, the one I use to remind her that she's saying quiet things too loud.

On the way over to Rene's I stick my head into the free clinic. There's a basket of condoms on the counter nine days out of ten, and you can take as many as you want for free. It's there, so I duck in and grab a handful, six or seven, and stick them in the pocket of my duster.

The woman at the counter has a modern hairstyle, about two inches long and all moussed back in waves. She smiles at me.

In a kind of purposely singsongy voice, I say, "Thank you."

"S'what they're there for," she says, purposely imitating my song voice.

I try to think of a way to get to Rene's without going by the leather store. There are lots of ways, but they all have me walking a little farther. And that's stupid, I decide. What am I, a little kid? I can stand to see something it hurts to want. I can see it and then just keep walking. It happens to lots of people every day. We all survive.

But when I pass the store, I don't just keep walking. It stops me dead, like seeing an old flame step out of a cab on a busy street. And once I'm stopped I stay stopped a minute, and I look at the duster coat. And I make the mistake of thinking about going to Rene's wearing that coat. It would be so different. It would be better even than it is now. He would look at me and see things he never saw before. I would be just as big as Rene and have just as much power, and we would have to find new games to play, ones that reined in both of our powers so we didn't both get burned to a crisp by all that self-satisfied cool.

The guy in the store is not the same guy as yesterday. He's a little older, maybe forty, with silvery hair and heavy black eyebrows. And a weird kind of male-pattern baldness that leaves one little hank of hair all alone by itself on his upper forehead, like an island. I'm so busy thinking about the duster coat and Rene and the new games that it takes me a minute to realize he's checking me out. I look him in the eye and drink in all that raw approval. And I almost wish the opportunity hadn't presented itself. I know in a flash that I probably—potentially—could get that coat. But I am not going to bend over for it. I refuse to bend over to get that coat because then every time I wear that coat, instead of feeling like the king, I'll feel like a guy who bent over. Instead of men crossing the city to fall down at my feet, I'll be picturing men crossing the city to tell me to bend over. I shake my head at him and walk on.

Over my shoulder I hear his voice. He's come out onto the street to call after me. "Hey, kid," he says. "Where ya going, kid?"

I'm going to Rene's.

"Jordan," Rene says. "My man."

I am struck dumb, as always, by how gorgeous he is. He's standing at the door in just a pair of jeans. He lifts weights, and his chest has great definition. And not one single hair. Not even around his nipples. He has a little skinny goatee, jet-black. He is Hawaiian and Nicaraguan, very dark and smoky and dangerous and gorgeous, and sometimes I just can't believe my own luck. Actually, every time. I just can't believe it.

"Business or pleasure?" Rene asks, stepping back to let me in.

"Maybe both," I say. "Maybe a little of both."

Then I know again how bad I need that coat, because I feel how it would be to stand in his one-room studio with the collar up and the sleeves pushed up to my elbows, saying, Maybe a little of both. That's the real me. I have to find a way to step up to what I know I could be.

"Which comes first?" he says, but he's already peeled my coat off onto the floor and he's unbuttoning my shirt, and then I couldn't talk if I wanted to. His arms are around my waist and he picks me up so my feet are an inch off the ground and he puts me down on his big bed.

Rene doesn't do this with just anybody. Lots of guys come by here to get work or do business, and Rene doesn't take them all into his bed. It reminds me that I'm right about what and who I think I am.

"I need some more work this week," I say. "Only nothing too dangerous."

Rene laughs at me. We're lying on his bed and he's on his back with my head on his chest, so my head bounces up and down when he laughs at me. "You always say that, my man. You say you need cash, but you're afraid to get busted. You want work with no risk. I got no work with no risk. You don't make a hundred dollars running an errand if there's no risk."

"What do you have, then?"

"Maybe some package deliveries. Next week."

"How much?"

"One-fifty each. Special for you. That's top dollar, my man."

"What's in the packages?"

"For one-fifty, you don't get to ask. That's what all the money's for. For a guy who ain't afraid to get busted and knows better than to ask."

"I'm sorry," I say.

"You're learning," he says. "You'll learn. You want the job or not?"

"I just can't afford to go to jail."

"Who would look after Chloe." He says it like a flat sentence, not like a question. He says it like criticizing me, throwing my own words in my face so I can get a good look at them. See how wrong they are. "Let her fall, Jordan. She ain't you."

"Yeah, she is," I say, and sit up and reach for my shirt. "Sure she is."

"You want the work?"

"How long do I get to decide?"

"Day after tomorrow. I don't hear from you by then, I make other arrangements."

"I'll think on it."

"You do that, my man. You think hard. Think what you want in this life. Don't throw a good life away."

When I get back to the Chock full o'Nuts, Chloe is AWOL.

"Shit," I say out loud. "Shit, shit, shit. Shit."

It races through my mind that maybe we'll never meet up again, and then I can take dangerous work, or even get a day job, and live more like other people do. But I don't really want her to be gone. I just run through the advantages of having it forced on me.

I ask the waitress which way she went, how long ago. She looks at me like, What am I, a friggin' detective service? But she doesn't say any of that. Just shrugs.

I walk out to the street again. Listen to the traffic noise and take a deep breath of carbon monoxide. Then I think, maybe she went to the leather store to look in the window. Maybe she even went to the leather store thinking I'd be there, looking in the window.

She's not there. Just the guy with the hair island, who recognizes me immediately and looks elated to see me again. He waves me in. I shake my head. He waves again. No, really. Come in. I shake my head again. I can tell I'm inflaming his passion every time I say no.

Then I think, at least I'll touch that coat. Try it on. That will be a moment, anyway. Something I can go back to in my head just before sleep tonight. I go inside.

Guy says, "You like that coat, huh?"

"It's a pretty nice coat," I say.

"That would look great on you." He takes it off the half-mannequin. I drop my own duster coat to the floor. "Come over here by the mirror," he says.

We walk toward the back of the store. He helps me into the coat like gentlemen did for ladies in the fifties. Or so I hear. He's standing behind me, his eyes on me in the mirror.

I look at myself. I'm everything I thought I would be. I'm everything I always knew I could be. I never should have put it on. I know that now. It sinks into my stomach like a heavy meal I forgot to chew. I can't take it off now. If I take it off, I'll never be me again.

I turn the collar up. Roll the sleeves back two turns. Push the sleeves up to my elbows.

The guy is smoothing it down in the back, over my ass. Like leather needs plenty of smoothing; sure, we all know that. I feel his hands at my waist. He moves up a little closer behind me. Then, when I don't move away, a lot closer.

"We can get you into this coat," he says. "At a price you can afford."

"I don't have any money."

His eyes are on mine in the mirror. "We can get you into this coat," he says.

I know now I have to take it off. Because he wants to get me into it all right, but first he wants to make it mean all the wrong things to me. One way or the other this feeling will be over.

"Let me show you something in the back room," he says, and he turns his back to me and walks away. As he ducks behind the curtain I think, just for a minute, that he'll go back there and trust me to follow. I wonder if I could outrun him.

But then he sticks his head back out and looks at me. "Coming?"

I duck back behind the curtain. It's like a stockroom back there, and he's leaning against some cartons, smiling at me.

"Bet the owner would be pissed about this," I say.

He laughs. "Honey, I *am* the owner."

"Ah. Well. That's handy. Thing is, I'm not willing to bend over for this coat. If I'd do it for anything, I'd do it for this coat. But as it turns out, I'm just not willing."

He doesn't stop smiling. "Would you go down on your knees for that coat?"

And it's a question I can't answer right off the bat. And the more I don't answer, the more we both know it's a possibility. I'm too flexible right now for my own good.

Then I make a decision what to do, and it makes my heart jump. When I walk up close to him, I wonder if he can hear it. My heart. I feel like I can hear it. Like it might give me away.

I unzip his pants and he stands up straight so I can take them down around his ankles. All the way to his shoes. And I go most of the way down with them. So it looks like I really will end up on my knees.

Then I run faster than I ever have in my life.

I shoot through the curtain and out the door of the shop. I swing right and pray I can hit the corner before he sees which way I've gone. At the corner I turn and look over my shoulder to see if he's out yet. He's not. But I should look where I'm going because I slam into a lady.

"Hey!" she says.

I turn the corner and think I'm home free, but then I hear him behind me.

"Little son of a bitch," he yells. "No way you get over on this one, you son of a bitch."

I'm running fast and the leather coat is flying out behind me, and I realize I look dignified running in this coat. I don't feel like a sneak thief—even though just at the moment I am that exactly. I feel like Superman. I look dramatic, I just know it, the way it flows out behind me like a cape. I look like I was born to move just like this, and maybe I never need to stop.

"You little son of a bitch," he yells, "I'll make you sorry you were ever born."

As I swing into an alley I think, Asshole, you're years too late.

I look over my shoulder and he has his pants up, but his fly is still open. And he's slowing down. He's not yelling at me anymore because he can't spare the wind. His face is red and his hair is flapping and I know I'm home free. I'm younger than he is, and I have this magic coat. I'll run forever and he'll wear down.

At the end of the alley I know I'll have to make a choice. If I go right, I'll pass the restaurant again—the one where Chloe is supposed to be. And what if she's there this time? I don't want to meet up with her until this is over. I don't want to draw her into this. I stretch closer to the street, already prepared to go left, and here comes Chloe. Wandering into the alley.

"Run, Chlo!" I grab her by the wrist as I fly by, spin her around in the right direction.

But, Chloe being Chloe, I look back and she's just standing there, looking confused. A split second later the guy catches up with her. I can see he couldn't have gone ten steps farther. I was

45

home free. Damn it, I was home free. Goddamn you, Chloe, you always do this to me. I was home free. This was working and you messed it up. Damn you, Chlo.

He has one of her hands twisted behind her back now, and one arm across her collarbone.

I just made a huge mistake. Because if I hadn't stopped, if I had kept running, he wouldn't have known she was anything to me. He would have nothing. Now he has everything. Now the whole thing just flipped over. It seems shocking to think I could lose a battle in this incredible coat. How can I look this great and lose?

"Friend of yours?" he asks. He's barely able to say it, he's so out of breath. I resent people who can afford to get out of shape like that.

Then Chloe does what I could have predicted Chloe would do. She bites him. Sinks her teeth into his arm and doesn't let go. I am here to testify: Chloe bites hard. Nobody wants to know how hard Chloe bites if she gets it in her head to. Nobody deserves to find out.

The guy screams, spins her away from him. Slaps her hard across the face.

That's when I know I have to hurt him.

They're deep into the alley now, Chloe kind of pulling him along. He's got hold of her wrist and he's twisting it, and he has his back turned to me. For one split second of fatal mistake he abuses Chloe and turns his back on me all in the same breath. Funny how we do things before there's even time to think how it will turn out. I run back in.

There are garbage cans in the alley, so I go to pick one up. That's all it's going to be. I'm just going to bash him in the head with a can and go on my way. I think it'll be empty, or filled with something light. Well, truthfully, I don't think. My brain is all black and anyway there's no time.

The can I grab is like fifteen times heavier than I expected. God only knows what's in it, but I pick it up anyway. I have so much adrenaline, I can actually lift this thing. I have so much adrenaline that when I feel the muscles pulling in my armpits, down my rib cage, it seems like something unimportant happening far away. As it comes down on his head I know—before it even hits him—that it will probably break his neck. Something about the angle and the weight. I see that coming. But now it's gravity, and you can't stop gravity.

As he's lying facedown in the alley I look down and think, It was about Chloe. Not the coat. I wouldn't do that for a coat.

I don't know what I did to the guy. I probably never will. Maybe he'll wake up with a hell of a headache. Maybe he'll be in a wheelchair all his life, moving it around by blowing into a tube. Maybe I wasted him right on the spot. I just know I didn't do it for the coat.

I grab Chloe's hand and we run away. When we turn out onto the street I slow us down to a normal walk. "Just walk," I say. "Just act like everything's normal."

We walk block after block, saying nothing. We cross against lights. Stop traffic. Ignore the honking, the flipped fingers.

About a half mile from home Chloe says, "That got bad, Jordy."

"I know. I'm sorry."

"Why do things get really bad like that?"

"Chlo," I say, "I'll be goddamned if I know."

* * *

47

I leave Chloe and the coat in the cellar and go close the bank account. Take all the money back to the cellar in my sock. We never go into this cellar by daylight, but it doesn't seem to matter today, because we'll never come back here again. We roll our stuff into the blankets and tie them up tight. We sit with our backs up against the wall, waiting for dark to come.

"This is your lucky day, Chlo."

"It is? Why?"

"Because you always wanted to get out of the city."

"Where are we going?"

"I don't know. But I promise you we'll have either a lawn, some bushes, or a tree."

"Wow. That's pretty lucky."

I can't imagine I'll sleep while we're sitting there waiting to go. In fact, I can't imagine I'll ever sleep again. I think I'll just sit up for the rest of my life, my eyes getting redder and redder, staring off into space, wondering why things are like they are.

Then after a while Chloe pokes me. "You're snoring," she says. "Stop that."

On the walk down to the Port Authority, I hold Chloe's left hand. She has something clutched in her right, but I don't ask what. I figure she has a right to some privacy.

"This was a really bad day," she says.

"I know, Chlo. I'm sorry."

"But then it turned into my lucky day. It turned around and got good."

Her hand pulls away from mine, and she runs to a place under the street lamp. Stands in the round wash of light and dances. Spins around like a ballerina on her toes. Chloe is having one of her ballerina days. "Lawns," she says, and spins. "Bushes," she says, turning. "Trees."

On the word "trees" her right hand flies up and opens and a snowstorm of paper confetti sails. I watch it catch on the wind, settle at my feet. I nudge a piece with my foot. I pluck three or four pieces out of the air, out of my hair.

"Your house pictures, Chloe. You tore them up?"

"Won't need them anymore," she says.

I look down at my hand again, and there's one piece that wasn't torn from a newspaper or a magazine. The paper is too stiff. I look closely at it and see the carefully drawn head of a snake.

"My crown, Chlo? You ripped up my crown?"

"Won't need it anymore," she says.

Then she gives me back her hand and we walk.

THREE
JORDY'S HOMETOWN

The first place we go look at is a disaster. A basement apartment. It didn't say that in the ad. Also no lawn, no bushes, no trees.

The second one is a dream, though an unattainable one. I mean, for God's sake. I don't even have a job. And I never managed to hold one before. Not with Chloe to look after. So what we're doing here, I don't know. But we're here. Because I promised. And I already know Chloe is never going to want to leave.

It's a small apartment built into the back of this old guy's house. Two back bedrooms converted into a small unit. Hot plate only, but with a bath and shower. Furnished. And it's cheap. Really cheap. I forgot how cheap you can live in this town. When he tells me the price, I actually have that in my sock. So we could actually stay a month. Potentially, we could. Before it all falls down. The house is on a big lot with a lawn all the way around. Of course, the grass is getting brown now, with winter coming on. But Chloe doesn't seem to care. She seems to trust it to go green again. It's fenced all around, with bare rose-bushes against the fence every few feet. In the spring I'm sure it will be incredible, but I can't imagine we'll get to still be here by then.

There isn't a tree exactly, but in another way there is. The trunk is in the neighboring yard, but branches spill over the old man's driveway, dropping red-and-orange leaves and whirlybirds. That's what we used to call them when I was a kid. Whirlybirds. Those seedpods with tails. If you throw them up in the air, they spin like little helicopter rotors all the way down.

The old guy is showing me the apartment, and I look out the back window and there's Chloe in the driveway, picking up handful after handful of whirlybirds and throwing them into the air over her head. Laughing as they copter down all around her. How did she know that? I wonder. Maybe she grew up someplace with whirlybirds. The early part of growing up. I don't know how Chloe grew up. We never ask each other questions about the past. That's one of the reasons why this works.

The old man wanders over to see what I'm staring at. He walks like he has steel rods from his waist down, holding every-thing in line. He's really old. "She's an exuberant girl," he says. But he doesn't say it like an insult, so I decide he's okay.

"I think she likes it here," I say.

There's a dog run in the corner of the yard, with a red dog-house at one end. I don't notice it until a massively overweight, geriatric Doberman pinscher waddles out of the doghouse, through the open run gate, and waddles fast in Chloe's direction. Fast enough that I think he might think he's running.

"Shoot," the old guy says. "Thought I had 'im locked up." He runs for the back door, the private entrance to our—hopefully—new place. "Don't move," he yells to Chloe. "Just don't move a muscle. I'll come get 'im."

Chloe picks up another handful of whirlybirds and launches them. Then she sees the Doberman waddle-running in her direction, and she runs to him. Meets him halfway. Gets down on her knees and throws her arms around his neck. "Good dog," she says.

The good dog wags his stump of a tail.

Meanwhile, the old guy hasn't even made it off the stoop. "Well, I'll be darned," he says.

"I'm going to take the place," I say. And I hand him two hundred dollars from my sock.

"First and last plus a security deposit."

"Let me give you a deposit on it," I say. "I'll give you a hundred to hold the place, not rent it to anyone." I hold the money out to him again. I move it slightly, wiggle it back and forth. Like the guy's a cat, and I can make him jump for it. I don't know why I bother. I don't have last month's rent. I don't have a security deposit. I don't have a job. I must not have a brain in my head, leading Chloe to the land of lawns, bushes, and trees just long enough to make her never want to leave again.

He takes it. "I hold the place a week, tops. You lose your deposit if it doesn't work out."

I go out in the backyard to talk to Chloe, and the dog grabs me by the back pocket of my jeans. He's snarling, and he won't let go.

The old guy screams at him. "Out, Bruno! Bruno! Out!"

But Bruno's teeth remain in the "in" position. The guy has to come out and pull him off me. Lock him up in the pen. I look at the back of my jeans as best I can. I can see the holes his teeth made.

Chloe gives me a handful of whirlybirds. I see she expects me to throw them, so I do.

The old man has gone back in the house now, and the dog is snarling at me through the wire of his run.

"Good dog," Chloe says.

As we're walking up the driveway, Chloe says, "Wow. Your parents are rich."

"This might be bad, Chlo. Just so you know."

"What might happen?"

"My father might scream at me. Or he might even hit me."

"What do I do if he hits you?"

"Nothing. You do nothing. You just get out of the way and trust me to take care of it."

I knock on the door. I expected my stomach to be doing all these fluttery things, or cold things, or tight things, but instead I just have a spot right in the middle of me that feels dead.

My mother opens the door. It's a weekday morning, but every hair is in place, her makeup is perfect, her long shell-pink nails are perfectly manicured. I'm not surprised, because it always was that way. I'm just taking it in. I won't say her eyes go wide or she clutches her chest or any stupid things like that, because none of it happens anyway. A quick scared thing flits through her eyes, that's all. Then she puts it away again.

"Jordan. My God. Your father is right out in the garage. How is this a good idea?"

"Good to see you, too, Mom." I know, have always known, that this is the crucial moment. I might not even be allowed in. "Mom," I say. "This is Chloe."

I watch my mother's face for a minute, noticing—almost enjoying—how she despises moments like this. The kind where she's thrown completely off her stride, where her composure takes a step to the side and she has to scramble to find it again. There are things I still haven't forgiven her. More the things she allowed than the things she did, but some of both, I suppose.

"Can we come in for a minute?" She's still not ready to answer, so I just lead Chloe in. We sit down on the edge of the sofa, close together, holding hands.

Then I hear a new voice, one I didn't think to expect. It says, "Jordy?" And then I see her face, peeking around a potted plant. "Jordy, you're here. I heard your voice."

My mother says, "Go back to bed, pumpkin."

I say, "What are you doing home from school, peanut?" My sister is only nine. She was an accident. As far as my parents are concerned. I think she was a good enough idea.

"Her asthma is acting up," my mother says. As always, giving Pammy no room to speak. As always, discussing her like she at least isn't around. Maybe like she never was.

"Pammy," I say. "This is Chloe."

"Chloe." She makes it sound like a nice thing. She's standing off from the situation; she catches its volatility. There's still a potted palm between us, but I can see her thick bangs. She wears them long, almost over her eyes. When I was younger I wanted to say, Good luck, kiddo. Grow them as long as you want, but the world is still all right there to see. But I didn't say that. I did my best to be kind.

Chloe responds to the introduction by waving the way a prom queen waves from a parade float. She must be having a prom queen day, which is a new one on me.

"Pamela, I said go!" my mother shouts. Chloe jumps, and then the potted palm is empty.

"Mom, I'm going to make this quick. I'm going to get right to it. We have a chance to get on our feet and live in a decent place, but some things have come up that we didn't expect."

"You need money."

"I never hit you for college, I walked out of here with the clothes on my back." Actually, I walked out of the hospital with the clothes on my back, but why split hairs? "I never asked you for money, and if you help us out today, I promise I won't ask again."

She rises dramatically from her chair. "Well, the money was never the problem, Jordan."

She finds her purse on the wet bar and brings her checkbook back, opens it onto the coffee table. "I can give you a thousand. Any more and I'd need your father to sign. He won't, of course."

I shake my head. "We don't need that much. Another five hundred and we'd get the place."

She stares at me like I've just said something in Swahili. "We can spare it."

"I don't want to take any more from you than I have to."

She continues with the confused look for a beat or two. Then she writes out the check. I wait for some kind of comment. Like she might say, That shows a certain ethic on your part. Or, I'm glad you want to do as much on your own as possible. In other words, I never learn.

"You always were a stubborn boy." She holds the check out

to me and I take it. It's for a thousand. "Now for God's sake please go before your father—"

"He's in the garage? I'm going in there."

"Dear God, Jordan, no."

But I'm already up off the sofa. "Wait right here, Chlo. It's okay." I refuse to walk out of this place like a whipped puppy, my tail between my legs. At least, I refuse to do it again.

My father has a workshop in the garage. He restores cars. He could afford to pay somebody to restore them for him, but I guess that wouldn't be the same. Then he might have time to go in the house or something. I step into his shop, and he's working on the Stutz. All this time later, he's still working on the freaking Stutz. I don't know why I should be surprised. It just confirms my suspicion that he never wants to be done.

He's standing looking into the engine. Just looking. He has a vinyl drop cloth over the fender, and on top of this a cigar burns in an ashtray. I notice an absence of tools. Maybe he's too close to done, and he's reduced to staring. I also notice that his bald spot is gone. Then a moment later I realize it's just black. His hair is dyed jet black now, and he's using some product to make the bald spot black, too. If you look right at it, it's pretty obvious.

He could see me out of his peripheral vision, but he doesn't make it clear if he does or not. And I'm still not scared. I know, because I keep checking. But it's still just that dead spot.

After a minute he says, "The answer is no."

So I say, "What's the question?"

"Whatever the question is, the answer is no." He picks up the cigar and puffs furiously. The air all around his head fills with bluish smoke. He still won't look at me. "What'd you come for," he asks, "money?"

"Partly," I say, because I refuse to be cowardly with him.

He waits a moment, then says, "Uh-huh. Look, there's just too much bad blood between us."

"I know."

"Why'd you even come out here then?"

I don't bother to answer. I just leave. I know the answer, I just don't bother to tell him. Because I could. That's the answer. To prove that I could.

On the way down the front steps with Chloe I hear Pammy's voice again. "Jordy." I turn around and she's on the cold steps behind me in pajamas and bare feet. I walk back to her and stand a couple of steps down so we're the same height, looking each other in the face. "Take me with you, Jordy."

"I can't, peanut. I'm sorry."

"Why not?"

"Because I'm just barely keeping my own head above water here."

"Oh. Okay. Do me a favor, Jordy?"

"What's that, peanut?"

"Be okay."

"Okay," I say. "Okay, I'll really try. Will you do me the same favor?"

She doesn't exactly answer. Just says, "Bye, Jordy. Bye, Chloe."

Chloe does that parade wave again.

Then my mother comes down the stairs and grabs Pammy by

the arm and spins her around and sends her running back into the house with a swat on the butt. Like Pammy was three or something. "It's cold out here. Get in that house before you catch bronchitis again."

My mother turns back to me. She looks at me like she's seeing me differently. I'm out here in the bright daylight and she sees something she didn't see before. I expect her to say, Jordan. You're almost a grown man now. In other words, I never learn.

I guess I should have noticed she was looking at my forehead.

"You still have that scar," she says.

"I'll always have that scar," I say.

On the night of the first snow, we're in our new place. In a real bed, with a mattress and box springs. And on a frame, not even down on the floor. With sheets. There's a gas furnace, and it's kind of rattly and loud, but it really makes the place warm. There's a window right by the bed, and we're lying here, not quite asleep. I think we're both lying here just enjoying this. Just feeling how great it is to have sheets, heat. A bathroom five steps away.

I look out the window and it's snowing. Hard.

"Look, Chlo," I say.

Her head pops up and she watches the snow for a minute. Then she throws the covers back and runs out the back door, still in her nightshirt with her feet bare. I'm thinking maybe she's planning on making snow angels in her nightshirt, in which case she'll freeze. She'll get frostbite for real. I watch out the window and she runs across the yard to the dog run and opens it and Bruno comes waddling out to greet her. Then she brings him back into our apartment.

"What are you doing, Chlo? Bruno never gets to come in the house. You know that."

"He'll get cold."

"He'll also bite me."

"No, he won't. Watch." She leads Bruno by the collar over to our bed. "Bruno, this is Jordy. Be nice to Jordy. Give him your hand, Jordy."

Reluctantly, I hold one hand out for him to sniff. He sniffs it, licks it once, then flops down on the rug beside the bed with a deep sigh. Smart dog, I think. He knows if he bites me, he's back out in the snow.

Chloe climbs back into bed with me. Her feet are wet and freezing. I make her give them to me so I can rub them until they warm up. So she doesn't get frostbite.

"Chlo, that dog slept outside for years before you lived here."

"Yeah," she says. "But now I live here."

Bruno is already snoring. Also, it doesn't take long to discover that flatulence is a Bruno concern. But I know better than to complain. I snore sometimes, and Chloe doesn't make me sleep out in the snow.

It's a few months later. Nearly spring. I'm on my way to check on the old guy, who lets us call him by his first name now. Otis. I'm on my way to check on Otis, because it's my job. He's going downhill. Chloe is lying on the bed watching *I Love Lucy*. We have a TV now, but as far as Chloe is concerned, there's only one program on, ever. Everything else bores her to tears.

"I'm going to check on Otis now," I say.

"Check on Bruno, too. Okay, Jordy? Will you see if Bruno's okay?"

"Why? Doesn't he seem okay to you?"

"Not really."

"What's he doing?"

"Nothing. He's not doing anything. He just doesn't feel good."

"Well, he's an old dog, Chlo."

"He was old when I met him," she says. "Today he doesn't feel good."

Otis is asleep, and I have to shake him to wake him up. Even though it's only a little after seven.

"Oh, did I fall asleep?"

"Otis," I say. "I think there's a problem with Bruno."

"What kind of problem?"

This is a hard one to field. The kind that only Chloe could put her finger on. But after going out to check on Bruno, I agree. He's not himself at all.

"I'm not sure, Otis. But I think you need to look at him."

"I can't walk all the way out there."

"I could bring him in. If he could just come in this one time."

"Well, sure," Otis says. "If you think it's serious." He's caught the mood of concern from me now. It has him awake and he's worried. "You think it's serious, huh?"

"Yeah, I think so, Otis. I think he's . . ."

And then I can't bring myself to say it. Which is funny, because I faced death every day for years. I came within an inch of it, right before I left this town, and I recently returned to the scene of the crime. I might have even dealt it out to somebody else. But right now, tonight, I can't make myself say the word.

"I think he's in trouble," I say.

❋ ❋ ❋

When I get back out to Bruno's run, it's dark and still pouring rain. At first I can't find him. At first I think he's just up and disappeared. Like someone or something beamed him out of here. But I do find him in time. But of course by the time I find him I'm cold and soaked to the skin.

He's managed to crawl into the narrow space between his doghouse and the fence. And there's no getting in there after him. I have to move the doghouse aside. I have to pull it into the center of the run. It's been at the end of the run for a long time. It was comfortable there. It had dug a rut for itself. Now I'm cold, wet, and out of breath.

"Bruno," I say. His head doesn't even come up.

As I take hold of his collar it occurs to me that he might bite. Even though he hasn't bitten me for a long time. Instead he just turns his big eyes up to me. Opens his eyes to the rain. Gives me this look, like, Do I have to, Jordan? I'm tired. Couldn't I just stay here?

I encourage him to take a couple of steps. He does. Two. Exactly. Then he goes into a sprawl, each leg pointing a different direction, like Bambi on the ice. Except when Bambi did it, it was cute. I give up and carry him.

Chloe is standing at the front door to Otis's house, holding the door open for me.

"Get a blanket," I say.

She goes to find one. I stand in the entryway holding Bruno. We're both dripping buckets of water onto the mat. Muscles in my back are straining. My arms are beginning to tremble.

"Hurry up, okay, Chlo?"

I can't bring myself to set him down on the carpet because he's covered with mud.

"I don't even know where Otis keeps blankets. Where do you keep blankets, Otis?"

"Hall closet," Otis calls. After a moment I hear the rhythmic scuffling of his walker.

Chloe comes running back with a blanket and throws it down like a nest on the carpet. "I'm putting it here by the fire, Jordy. You'll have to light a fire."

I set Bruno on the blanket. Just for a second my back screams louder than it did when I was holding him. Why didn't somebody put that dog on a diet?

We look up, and Otis is shuffling across the carpet. His face doesn't look like his face. It looks like the face of someone else, someone softer and more open. It takes him a minute or two just to cross the living room. Bruno watches his progress without even raising his head.

"Oh," Otis says. "Oh. Oh, Bruno. He is in bad shape, isn't he?"

"Light a fire, Jordy," Chloe says.

"Should I take him to the vet, Otis?"

"No, don't," Otis says. "He's dying. Vet hasn't got a cure for that yet."

"No, don't," Chloe says. "He wants to be at home, Jordy. He wants you to light a fire."

Otis and I are having a moment. We're sitting on the couch together, have been for hours. Watching Chloe and the dog.

They're on the other side of the room, by the fireplace. Every now and then I've been getting up to feed more wood into the fire. Chloe didn't raise her head the last time. Maybe she's gone to sleep. We know Bruno is sleeping. We can hear him snore all the way over here.

Chloe dried him off with towels. Put another blanket over him. Me, I had to run around to our apartment in the rain to dry off and put on warm clothes. Then again, this isn't my last night on the planet. She's lying with him the way she sleeps with me every night. Draped over him like she's looking for the doorway into his skin. I watch rain stream down the windows in the dark. It gives me a feeling that the whole world is taking a moment to be sad.

Otis says, "Nobody ever loved my dog before but me." He says it quietly. It's a moment between us, one not designed to reach all the way to Chloe, who has better things to do anyway. "Nobody ever even liked my dog before but me."

"I like Bruno," I say.

Otis looks over at my face, a serious taking-in. It occurs to me briefly that Otis's last night on the planet might not be a long way off, either. "I guess you might," he says. "Yeah. I guess by now you do. He's not the most likable dog who ever lived."

"He grows on you."

"I was wrong about you. You turned out to be all right after all. When I first met you, I had my doubts."

"Both of us?"

"No, you. I always liked her. Granted, she's not the sharpest tool in the shed. Now, I can say that, because you know I love the girl."

"She's funny," I say. "Lots of things she can't do as well as we could. But then other things she does better."

"Like what?" Otis asks. He's sleepy. He's a little boy past his bedtime. He yawns.

"Music. Art. Other things. She's the one who knew Bruno was sick."

"Not sick," Otis says. "Dying. Call it what it is."

Just as he finishes that sentence we hear one last loud, strange snore; then the snoring stops. Stays stopped. Chloe picks up her head. Her face is all lit up, beaming. She's looking at a spot in the corner of the room, high, near the ceiling.

"Wow," she says. "Bruno," she says. "Good dog."

I look over at Otis and he's watching her closely. Intensely, like he sees something he never saw before. I guess I could be wrong. If I'm right, he never says what it is he sees.

In the morning, before anyone else is awake, I bring the wheelbarrow around to the front porch. Then I go into the living room and lift Bruno for the last time.

"What are you going to do with him?" Chloe asks. I don't know she's awake until she asks that.

"I'm going to bury him in the backyard."

"Is that what Otis said he wanted?"

"Yes."

"Good. That's what Bruno said he wanted, too."

While I'm digging, Chloe squats with her back against the fence, drawing something with her markers. She still has that same pad and markers. When I give Chloe something as a present, she doesn't lose it, and she's slow to use it up. It's like she saves it for special occasions.

The rain's let up for a time, but it's left the ground soft. I also think there's more on the way, but it was nice enough to give us this break. Give us a chance to bury our dead.

Chloe says, "Jordy? What does it mean to die?"

"I don't really know," I say. "I know what it means for the

people who don't die. It means we never get to see that person again. But I don't know what it means for the one who dies. That's not very much to know, I guess."

"It's okay, Jordy. You did fine. Is Otis going to die?"

"We're all going to die, Chloe."

"Is Otis going to die soon?"

"Yeah, probably. Pretty soon."

"Are you going to die soon?"

I miss one shovel motion, the way a heart will miss one beat worrying about something else. I wonder if that heartbeat ever gets made up again. If we ever get that back.

"No. Why would I die?"

"I don't know. I was just thinking, what would I do if you did?"

"I won't."

"Promise?"

"Nobody can really promise that, Chlo. But there's no reason why I should die any sooner than you do."

"Good," she says. "Good. I would hate it if you died sooner than me. I would hate that." Then she draws in silence for a while.

I look at her face and try to put my finger on something. Something that's there, but never was before. One of those things Chloe has always been missing, yet a trace of it is hanging around somewhere. But I'm not even sure what it is.

When the hole is about three feet deep, I tip Bruno into it. Then I get down there with him and arrange him a little so he looks more comfortable. So I don't have to picture him doing a bad Bambi imitation for all of eternity.

I'm about to throw the first shovelful of dirt onto him when Chloe yells, "Wait!"

She's done with her drawing now, but she takes the scissors and begins cutting. She ends up with a big round disc of paper with a little eye hook on top, like a dog tag. She lets it flutter down and land on Bruno's side.

"Okay, now," she says.

I look down and see she's made Bruno a giant dog tag that says GOOD DOG, with the word BRUNO written in vertically, twice. The two O's in the words BRUNO are shared with the first O in GOOD and the O in DOG. It occurs to me that I never would have known Bruno was a good dog if Chloe hadn't told me.

As I shovel dirt onto it, I actually notice a lump in my throat. I haven't cried for so long. I can't even remember the last time. Maybe I'm regaining my ability to feel things. Which I absolutely refuse to do until someone can guarantee me it won't be retroactive.

"Jordy," Chloe says. "You're crying. That's so nice."

In the middle of the night I wake up and Chloe is not draped all over me. Not in the bed beside me. I crane my neck to look in the bathroom, but the door is open and I can see she's not there. The rain has come back. I can hear it pounding on the roof. I'm so sleepy, and I'm really hoping this won't get too complicated. Then again, it's Chloe.

I look out the back window and there she is, squatting by the grave in the pouring rain, her knees doubled up under her wet nightshirt, her hair plastered down all around her head. If I leave her out there, she'll freeze. If I go out and get her, I'll freeze.

I go out and get her.

I put one hand on her shoulder. "Chlo—"

She jumps up and grabs me. The way I'd expect her to grab on if she was about to fall off a twenty-story building. Then again, maybe she is, and I'm just too blind to know it.

"I'm scared, Jordy."

"I know. I can tell. It's okay. Are you scared of me dying?"

"I don't know."

"Are you scared I'll leave you?"

"I don't think you'd do that."

"What are you scared of?"

"I don't know."

"What does it feel like? Tell me what it feels like, Chlo."

She never answers.

The rain is running into my eyes, and the cold is setting up a slight tremble right in the center of me. Once upon a time that would've been the only way I could find the center of me. But tonight I'm unfortunately aware of its location.

She's shaking a little bit again, even though it's not cold in here. This is definitely not about cold. Something rattled her deeply, and I can't get in to know what, because I can't get deeply into Chloe. Nobody can. As far as I know. I didn't even know Chloe had a deep place to get into.

I lie with her while she goes to sleep. She seems to have exhausted herself with that sudden burst of terror. Terror. Chloe. Chloe's never scared of anything.

But anyway, she's going off to sleep now, and it seems to be over.

It has to have been Bruno's death. What else could it be? The worst is over now. New York is just a bad memory, Bruno is buried, Chloe and I are slightly battered but still here.

We're safe and warm, we're together, we're still here.

Whenever I see something raise its head for the first time and then settle again, I never like to think it's the tip of an iceberg. I always like to figure it's a one-time thing that'll never be seen or heard from again.

I wake in the middle of the night to find Chloe sitting up on the edge of the bed. Caught in the act of not sleeping. She has her back to me, but the minute I wake up, she turns to look, as if she can hear my eyes open. Or maybe she's been looking at me a lot. I don't know.

"When Otis dies," she says, "we're going to need a whole new plan."

I'm surprised. I didn't know Chloe even thought about plans. I thought she left all the planning up to me.

In the morning she's sort of okay and sort of not. She's not shaking, not outwardly scared, but there's something. Some little shadow behind her eyes where there used to be clear skies every day. We lie together for a long time, and I'm half wondering if Otis is okay. But I'm half wondering if Chloe is okay, too, so I put off checking on Otis. Poor Otis. Just lost his best friend. I wonder if that'll make him less likely to stick around, like the husbands and wives that die within a few months of each other.

As if she were hearing me think, Chloe says, "When Otis dies, where will we live?"

"I don't know, Chlo."

"Who gets the house when he dies? Maybe they won't let us

live here. Maybe they'll sell the house and the person who buys it'll have a big family and want the whole house."

"Let's cross that bridge when we come to it, Chlo."

"What bridge?"

"Not a real bridge. It's an expression. It means don't worry about a problem until it comes."

I realize briefly why I never used that phrase with Chloe before. Because, as far as I can remember, this is the first time she ever crossed a bridge we hadn't yet come to.

I go up front after a while to check on Otis. When he sees me coming he grabs a tissue and wipes at his face, roughly, like he can still make it look like something more manly than crying.

"Thanks for giving him a good proper burial," he says.

"No problem, Otis. He deserved it."

Then we sit quietly for a moment, and I'm not sure what to say. I'll get up and make his breakfast soon, but in the meantime it feels like something more needs saying.

Otis nods a moment. His eyes are puffy and swollen. "I know you think I'm a stupid old man, but I know what's what. And I'm not sure she's so stupid."

"Yeah," I say. "I know."

"You act like you buy it."

"I act like it's the truth most of the time. Because most of the time it's the truth. But when she wants to be smart she just is."

"Which means she just is. All the time."

We sit quietly for a minute. I'm wondering if I should say more.

"There was a doctor in New York," I say, "who thought it might be like a defense for her. He barely knew her, so I couldn't figure out why he said that. It sounded like a weird thing for him to say out of nowhere at the time. But he still could have been right."

"She had a hard life?"

"Very."

"For example . . . ?"

"I really don't know what happened before I met her. Except that it was bad." I know it involved a lot of rape, but I can't bring myself to say that out loud to Otis. "What's beginning to worry me . . ." Then I decide not to finish that thought.

"What?" Otis says.

"Nothing. What do you want for breakfast?"

"What's beginning to worry you?"

"Nothing. How about oatmeal with walnuts?"

"Spill it out, boy."

Shit. "Okay. I asked the doctor if it was something she might get over. You know, if somebody cared enough to give her a better life and make her feel secure. He didn't know. And I didn't know if I was willing to try. But now that we're together, and she's getting more secure, I worry that . . ." I haven't even formed this into words yet in my head, and now I'm getting ready to do it out loud. No turning back. "What if all that simpleminded stuff starts falling away and then she just has no defenses?"

While nobody is answering I listen to his bedside clock ticking. How he can even sleep with such an enormous ticking, I'll never know.

After a time Otis says, "Oatmeal with walnuts'll be just fine."

I get up to go make it for him. Just as I'm leaving the room, he says, "You can't just keep her unhappy."

I stop with one hand on the door frame. "I know."

"So there's no way to go but forward. Cross that bridge when you come to it."

Good advice, I think.

FOUR

DEFENSELESS

I make Otis his supper at five p.m. sharp, just the way he likes it. Grilled cheese sandwich, carrot sticks, creamed corn, chocolate pudding cup. If that sounds cruel, I should note that this is Otis's idea of the perfect meal. I leave Chloe to handle the dinner dishes, and I go off to work.

Chloe and Otis babysit each other while I wait tables. Maybe I'm making too much out of too little, but the more time goes on, the more I feel like I can't trust Chloe to be alone. I mean, I never really left her alone much, because she might wander off or do something stupid. But she's been different lately, switching suddenly into these out-of-nowhere moods that feel very frightened or very dark. So now I'm thinking she might do something *really* stupid. But I can't put my finger on why I think that. I just feel better when she and Otis have each other.

The reason I'm working a job is because Otis is going down-hill fast.

For quite a while now his sister has paid us a little each month to look after him, and we also get the apartment for free. And we've gotten by just fine. But when Otis dies, she'll sell the house, and we'll be out on the street. She's told us quite frankly that she'll put it up for sale immediately. So I've been hustling very hard for tips and putting money aside.

We all hope that Otis will live forever, but it just doesn't seem to be going that way.

Everybody dies. Even Chloe knows that.

I work at a fancy dinner restaurant downtown. I have to park Otis's old truck two or three blocks away because it doesn't have much muffler. It's one of those restaurants that's all about ambi-ence. I have to be part of it. Or at least not detract.

Every now and then we get a family or a business dinner, but mostly it's couples. They make me feel sad for reasons I can't en-tirely pin down.

But tonight there's a couple that breaks through that fog. By being more like me. A nice-looking guy in his late forties with a pretty young guy about my age who is obviously his date. They both order the lobster. I get one meal per shift but I can't have filet mignon or lobster. I could if I had a financially stable boyfriend in his late forties, but I don't. I have a noisy old pickup that's not mine, a cranky old man who's dying on me, a job wait-ing tables, and Chloe.

After I take their order I slip into the bathroom and lock my-self in and look at my own face in the mirror. To see if I'm still pretty. Not enough, I guess. The scar on my forehead is ugly. It detracts from the overall picture. Breaks up the purity of the scene, making me seem like damaged goods. And my eyes look old to me, older than I really am. I look tired.

I guess I knew I was tired. I just didn't know I looked it.

Later, after we close, I get to eat. My one really great meal of the day. I usually choose the salmon, because that's Chloe's favorite. I always bring half home in a doggie bag for her. I sit outside on the patio to eat, even though it's a little cold out. I figure that way none of the other waiters will come sit with me. But tonight Marlon does, because he wants to smoke.

He has a half-finished bottle of wine that he rescued before it could get thrown out. He gestures in my direction, offering to fill my empty water glass. He's pretty enough, and he has a look like nothing could tire him out. Whatever it is, he could get the best of it. At least, that's what it says in his eyes. Sometimes I think people lie to the world with their eyes. If they still can.

I shake my head.

"Don't drink?"

"No."

"Don't like it?"

"Oh, I like it fine," I say. "I just don't start because if I start I don't stop."

"So? Don't stop. A bunch of us are going out partying, why don't you come? You look like you could use a little R and R."

"No. Sorry. My . . . wife is waiting up for me at home." It's easier to lie.

"So? Bring her."

"Oh. No. I don't think so. She's been kind of . . . She's not really much into partying. She's been kind of depressed."

"Oh," Marlon says. "Sorry."

I never really liked Marlon. Or any of the others, really. I'm sure they're okay people, but my world and their worlds don't intersect at any point. We really have nothing in common.

I pack up half my salmon to take home to Chloe.

Marlon says, "Just so you don't end up down there with her."

"I'm fine," I say. And I am. I'm strong. I'm pretty enough. Nothing tires me out. Whatever it is, I can get the best of it. "I'm just going to go home."

When I get home, I go into the main house first. Chloe is asleep on the end of Otis's bed, curled up like a good dog. Otis is wide awake. Which is weird, because it's after eleven. Otis is never awake when I get home. Sometimes he's not even awake when I leave. On his dinner tray is a card-sized envelope with a little pre-made bow stuck on it. I have no idea what that's about and it doesn't seem right to ask. Maybe Chloe gave him a present. She's like that.

Otis looks a little ruffled, so I sit on the edge of his bed and we chat.

"Something wrong, Otis?"

"Oh, the girl and I just had us a long talk. Hard to go to sleep after that."

"Not for her, apparently."

We both look down at her for a moment, watching her sleep.

Then Otis says, "Get her some help, son. Professional help. And do it soon."

I feel a cold pit in my belly because he knows something I don't. "What happened, Otis?"

"Nothing. We just talked. But I'm telling you, she needs help. The stuff she's seen and the stuff has happened to her, there's no way she could hold that up all by herself."

"She told you about the time before I met her?"

"From the time she was born till the day she hooked up with you. Everything."

"She never told me any of that."

"She's got her reasons, boy. She knows once you lay some stuff like that on a person they just don't set it down again. The more that person loves her, the harder it sits."

"Tell me, Otis."

"Nope. I swore I wouldn't. I'm just telling you this. Get her some help to deal with this stuff. She can't do it alone, and you're not enough, either, no matter what you might want to think. You can get some help on the money. You can call the county, tell 'em you're low income. There's help out there."

"Okay, Otis. If you think that's the best thing."

"Promise me, Jordan."

He never called me by my name before. As far as I can remember. This is a first.

"Okay. I promise. I'll get her some professional help."

Otis sighs, and the sigh seems to shrink him two or more sizes. "Okay, good. Now, here, this is for you. But you can't open it till you get back in your own place." He hands me the envelope with the bow. Chloe must've helped him decorate.

"Okay, Otis, thanks."

I put it in my shirt pocket, squashing the bow slightly. But I can't bring myself to take the bow off. If it wasn't important, they wouldn't have conspired to put it there. I pick up Chloe in a fireman's carry and head out of Otis's room.

"Jordan," he says. "You're okay. I'm sorry what I said, not being sure about you at first. You're a good boy."

"Well, that's okay, Otis. I wasn't sure about you at first, either. But I like you fine now."

He nods and closes his eyes.

Chloe wakes up when I try to undress her and get her into bed.

"Jordy," she says, "did you open your present?"

"Not yet. I will in a minute. How come you told Otis all that stuff you'd never tell me?"

"He told you all that stuff? He promised he wouldn't tell you!"

"He didn't tell me what the stuff was, just that you told him stuff from before I met you."

"Oh. Good."

"How come you told him when you wouldn't tell me?"

"Because he's going to die pretty soon. So then there still won't be anybody in the world besides me who knows all those secrets. Open your present, Jordy."

I open the envelope. Inside is the title to the old Chevy pickup. Otis has signed off on its ownership in a careful, fussy old man's hand. I stare at it for a long time, turn it over in my hands. Just tonight I was feeling sorry for myself because all I had was somebody else's pickup truck. The whole time, the truck was actually mine. I just didn't know it yet.

I look up to say something to Chloe, but she's fallen back asleep.

In the morning I go up to Otis's room, open all the curtains.

"Wake up, Otis," I say. "I have to tell you something. Do me a favor and don't even look at me while I tell you this, because it's hard. I'm not good at saying thank you to people. Maybe because I'm not good at feeling like I owe anybody. I've always gotten by on my own. No help from anyone. But I appreciate what you did. I never had my own transportation before. It makes me feel freer, like there's more I could do. Less helpless, you know?" I allow a pause, in case Otis wants to interject. He doesn't. He's probably no better at being thanked than I am at thanking. "Anyway, thanks. It means a lot. Really." Another long pause. I look over at Otis, who still has his eyes closed. "Otis?"

I go over to his bed, lean over, touch his forehead.

Cold.

"Tell me again why we have to do this, Jordy?"

"Because I promised Otis before he died."

"Oh."

Now I'm glad I did, because that's a tough one for Chloe to fight.

She doesn't want to go see the psychiatrist, and I don't really blame her. How will she tell all that stuff to a total stranger? She can't even tell me. Maybe if I could convince her that the psychiatrist was about to die.

I wait in the lobby on a hard wooden bench for fifty minutes.

Chloe comes out with a little slip of paper in her hand. We walk out into the street.

"Can I see that, Chloe?"

"Sure. We have to go to the drugstore on the way home. Can we afford this?"

She hands me the paper, and I see it's a prescription for Zoloft.

"Well, sure, if this is what the doctor says you need."

"She said I have to have it because I might want to hurt myself."

"Why does she think you would want to hurt yourself?"

"Because I told her sometimes I want to hurt myself."

"Oh. We can afford them. We just will."

"I told her I can't swallow pills but she wouldn't listen."

"We'll practice," I say. "I'll help you learn how."

We start with something cheap and easy. An aspirin. Because it becomes clear early on that she's going to saturate and gag up and generally ruin at least several dozen, and her Zoloft isn't cheap. I try to teach her to take big swallows of water, then drop the pill in, throw her head back. I tell her it will slide down almost without her feeling it.

But apparently that's something like telling her she won't even see the needle.

Taking the pills makes her nervous, and her gag reflex gets so acute that she can—and does—gag on plain water. She begs me to stop making her try. I tell her no, now that I know that she might want to hurt herself, I can't let her stop trying. She has to swallow the pills.

She cries, and we put the lesson off for an hour or two.

The second time, she throws up before the pill hits her lips. I try to be calm as I clean up.

The third time, she slides the aspirin into her mouth, swallows, and smiles.

"There," I say. "Was that really so hard?"

She smiles, and I see the aspirin clenched tightly between her front teeth.

*　*　*

Ever since the pills, Chloe has changed. Nothing pleases her anymore. She sleeps too much. She enjoys too little. I can't remember the last time we laughed about anything. She watches *I Love Lucy* and never so much as cracks a smile. She hates everything. Everything I ask of her is asking too much. And I'm not suggesting that the pills themselves have had a negative effect on her mood, because we haven't managed to get one down her yet.

"I only want you to take one," I say. "I just want you to try. Just to prove to yourself that you can. And until you do, you have to promise you won't hurt yourself."

"I promise I won't hurt myself. But I can't do pills. I can't."

"I'll crush it up and put it in some cherry-vanilla yogurt." Cherry-vanilla is Chloe's favorite.

Chloe says, "Then it won't taste like cherry-vanilla yogurt, it'll taste like pill. The reason I like cherry-vanilla yogurt is because it doesn't taste like pill."

Chloe has picked up one Zoloft and is holding it in her palm, looking at it. And looking at it. And looking at it. Like she expects it to evolve somehow. I bring her a glass of water. She puts the pill on her tongue. Takes a gulp of water. Swallows.

"Fabulous," I say.

Chloe shakes her head. Shows me her tongue. It's still on her tongue. At the last minute she must've chickened out. She takes five more gulps of water, chickening out every time.

Then there's only one gulp of water left in the glass. I hold her hand in case that will help her be brave. She takes the rest of the water, gulps, gags, and vomits the contents of her mouth and part of the contents of her stomach onto the table. Onto the other pills.

I have to throw them away and start all over again.

I'm sitting in a soft chair with arms, talking to Chloe's new psychiatrist. Dr. Reynoso. I can't believe I get a soft chair with arms. I feel lucky that this doctor works on a sliding scale, and that the fee slides down as low as it does. All the way down to meet us.

Still, the money is going out, only out. Nothing is coming in. No plan for how I can work without leaving Chloe alone. Everything is great except that we're headed for a wall.

Dr. Reynoso is in her sixties, wearing a burgundy pantsuit. It looks expensive. Other people must pay her a lot more.

"Chloe really likes you," I say.

"She says that?"

"Yeah. All the time."

"I'm surprised. She doesn't act like she does when she's here."

"She's not very trusting when I'm not around."

"Maybe you should be around during the sessions."

"No. That wouldn't help. She won't talk about her past around me because it would hurt me to have to carry all that. Also because I'm going to continue to be in her life. You have to be dying. How does she seem when she's here as far as . . . intelligence?"

The doctor shrugs. "Average, I guess. Maybe a little above."

"Oh." I sit quietly for a minute, rolling a little bit of jeans fabric between my fingers. Listening to the silence, knowing I'm seeing what Chloe sees and hearing what she hears during her sessions. "When I first met her she was really simple. I mean, actually like she was simpleminded. Sometimes she still is. You'd almost think she was retarded. It's like she just didn't understand anything but good things. Anything bad, she just didn't see it. She lived her whole life on a very childlike level. Still does sometimes. I mean, still does, mostly. Except, like . . . Well, like once when I was really sick. She did a lot of pretty complicated stuff to help me. And when Bruno died, her mood got really dark. And she never used to get dark, no matter what kind of crap was going on. Now it kind of comes and goes."

"And you really miss the simple side when it's away, right?"

I meet her eyes and then look down at my jeans again. "I didn't say that."

"Okay."

"I think I might've killed a guy once. I'm not sure. If I did, it wasn't on purpose. I'm not somebody who could do a thing like that on purpose, but sometimes things happen even when we didn't mean for them to." I had no idea that was about to get said.

"You want to tell me about it?"

"No, this shouldn't be about me. We're here to talk about Chloe."

"You must need to talk to somebody sometimes, though. It must be a lot of pressure for you. Always thinking about Chloe. Taking care of Chloe. What about your own needs?"

"Well, I'd have died if it wasn't for her, anyway."

"It's still got to be hard. Why don't you tell me about the time you might've killed somebody?"

"No. I don't want to talk about that. I have no idea why I brought that up."

"Because it weighs on your conscience. Obviously. Have you thought about turning yourself in?"

"I've thought about it, yeah. But I can't. Who would take care of Chloe? Let's get back to Chloe. Is she making any progress with you at all?"

"I wish I could say she was, Jordan. But she barely talks to me. There's a lot of dark stuff down there, and she won't even let me scratch the surface. I'd like to talk a little more with *you*, though."

There's a very obvious question here, but it takes me a while to get to it. So we suffer in this long silence. Well, I suffer, anyway. Do therapists suffer? I don't know, but probably not over stupid little things like silence. "To talk about Chloe? Or about me?"

"I was thinking we could talk about *you* sometime. How would you feel about that?"

Pretty much the way I'd feel about dying a slow, painful death. I'd rather drive my truck off a cliff. If I had a cliff. I'd rather spend the day with my father. "Fine," I say.

I'm feeling jumpy and I know Dr. Reynoso must see it. She keeps smiling at me like she sees it. I keep giving these one-word answers, and I have to stop that.

I'm thinking I'll just plunge in. Say what I need to say and get it off my chest. I'm not entirely sure I want to trust her. But I'm feeling desperate, like I have to trust somebody. And she seems like a better somebody than most.

"I'm worried that you're going to turn me in for what I did." There. I said it.

"No."

"Because I really don't see the point of me going to jail. It's not like society needs to be protected from me, because I would never hurt anybody. I mean, normally. And it's not even really like I need to be punished, because I've punished myself worse than what anybody else would do to me. And Chloe's the one who would really suffer. And she's the only one who didn't do anything wrong." Then I feel all those words sag and hover somewhere near the carpet, and they seem kind of pathetic. Especially since she said no.

"Okay. That's actually not what I was hoping we could talk about. I know it's a big issue to you, and you can talk about it if you want, but I was more interested in talking about you having a life of your own."

Now I feel fidgety again, and I wonder again if it shows. "Meaning . . . ?"

"Well. You said Chloe's not your girlfriend. But aren't you interested in having a girlfriend?"

"Oh. No. I mean . . . Well, what I mean is . . . I'm gay. Is the thing."

"A boyfriend, then."

Wow. That was weirdly easy. "You make it sound like no big deal."

"Lots of people are gay, Jordan."

"Not in my family."

"Is that why you're not interested in having a partner?"

I sigh. I wish I didn't have to talk about this. "Not really. It's more that the whole sex/romance thing wasn't going very well."

"Okay. But if you were trying to learn to play baseball or piano, and it wasn't going well, you'd have to practice, right? You couldn't just fix it by taking a break from it. I'm just concerned that you're devoting too much of your life to helping Chloe. I'd like to see you have more of a life of your own."

"Maybe after we get Chloe all squared away," I say.

Then a long silence falls. A very long silence. I know what I'm thinking, and I have a feeling she's thinking the same thing. Chloe? All squared away?

"Thing is," I say, "I wouldn't even have a life if it wasn't for Chloe. I mean, I would've died in that cellar in New York if she hadn't done something."

She lets that sink in for a minute. Even though we both know I've told her this before. "If she saved your life, Jordan, then she must want you to have it. I doubt she saved it so you could turn your back on it."

"I'll have to think about that," I say. I hear it, but right now I can't find room for it in my head. Right now, just filing it away for later is a strain.

After that I talk about the guy in New York. The guy from the leather store. Because she said I could. We don't really come to any conclusions about it, though. And I don't feel any better for talking about it.

I thought talking about stuff like that was supposed to make you feel better.

I know Chloe wants me to have my life. I know that. But do I want it? That's the tricky part of the equation.

Chloe tapes pictures up over the bed. That's another way for me to know that things are very wrong. There are no houses in the pictures. There are no lawns, no bushes, no trees. Every picture is a picture of the ocean. The beach. In two of them, people are riding horses.

We're lying in bed, waiting to go to sleep.

"Jordy? Where can you go and ride horses on the beach?"

"I'm not sure."

"Can you find out? Could you figure that out for us? 'Cause we're going to have to go somewhere that isn't here," she says.

In the morning we're kneeling on the bathroom floor again. The tiles are cold against my knees. I'm behind Chloe, holding back her hair. Now we've progressed to vomiting the medication in liquid form. I thought the liquid stuff would help. Not so much. She can still taste it.

I hate this. I hate this as much as she does, but I don't see what else we can do.

When I think she's done, I hand her a scrap of toilet paper so she can wipe off her lips. I hand her a glass of tap water so she can rinse out her mouth. She spits the water out into the toilet and flushes. Pulls me back down behind her and pulls my arms around her waist. I hold her tightly because she needs me to.

"Jordy," she says. "I don't want to do this anymore."

I felt this coming. I heard it creeping around the corner. Even though Chloe has never flat-out refused me anything—at least, anything with no needles involved—she was about to refuse me this, and I've known it for days. Just not what to do about it.

"You have to, Chloe."

"Why? Why do I have to?"

"So you won't want to hurt yourself. So you'll survive, and you can live a long time."

"Why would I want to live a long time like this?"

"You'll get used to taking it, Chlo."

"I don't think so."

She's right of course. With every passing day her gag reflex grows more emotional, more prepared. Now she can barely hold down a glass of water. And it's getting worse, not better. I'm the only one pretending it will get better.

"I've gone through a lot for you to have the medication, because it'll help you."

"It's not helping me very much so far."

"Well, I wanted it to."

"Well, maybe you didn't know it wouldn't make me happy."

"Please try to take it. For me. I want you to live a long time."

"I just don't believe like you do."

"About what?"

"I just don't believe the world is a nice place, Jordy."

We both fall silent for a long time. We're still on our knees on the bathroom floor, with my arms around Chloe's waist. It's a strange posture but at least I don't have to look her in the face. Because, truthfully, I'm not so sure I believe that, either.

As if she could hear that thought, Chloe says, "Are you sure you think the world is a nice place, Jordy?"

I really don't feel right lying to her.

"I want to," I say. "I want to believe that." We're quiet again for a minute. Her hair is close against my face, and it smells nice, like some kind of flowery shampoo. "It's a beautiful world," I say. "I'm not sure if it's always nice, but I know for a fact that it's beautiful."

"What's beautiful about it?"

"Lots of things. Mountains. Rivers. Oceans."

"I never saw an ocean."

"You're kidding. You lived in New York."

"But I never saw the ocean. I saw the river. It wasn't that pretty."

"Some rivers are, though. The Colorado River snaking through the Grand Canyon. That's beautiful."

"I never saw the Grand Canyon. I never saw the ocean. Except for that water where the big statue is. What's that called?"

"New York Harbor."

"Is that the ocean?"

"No."

"Is the ocean better than that?"

"Much."

"Good. 'Cause that isn't really so beautiful."

We get up off our knees. Mine are sore from the kneeling, and I can feel the little ridges etched into my skin from the edges of the tiles. I help her down onto the bed and lie down with her. She feels small in my arms, like she's shrinking her way out of here. I know we've reached the end of something. All my little prescriptions for her mental health. She just isn't having any more.

"Will the pills make me think the world is beautiful?"

"I'm not sure. Probably not."

"But you really think it is."

"Yes." I have to at least try. Or why would *I* even want to stay?

"Can't you show me what's so beautiful about it?"

"I'm not sure you can show that to somebody. I mean, you look at something beautiful and you may see it or you may not."

88

"So if I saw the Colorado River doing whatever you said it does in the Big Canyon, I wouldn't think it's beautiful?"

"No, you would. Anybody would. Some things everybody thinks are beautiful."

"Like what else?"

"Oh. Um. Niagara Falls. The Rocky Mountains. The ocean. The Painted Desert."

"Wouldn't showing me those things be better than the pills? Maybe the world really is beautiful and I just don't know it because I haven't seen those things yet."

I want to tell her there's more to it than that. That her depression is not about whether there are fine scenic sights, but whether people are decent or abusive, evil or kind. It's about whether the whole planet is fair, or even marginally safe. But I don't say that, because she's presented a possible plan of action. It's one I know probably won't work, but I want to cling to it. It's got to beat the hell out of lying here watching her shrink her way out of the world. If nothing else, it would fill our days with something better to do.

At least it wouldn't make things any worse.

"Maybe so," I say. "Maybe that's just the problem. Nobody ever showed you what a beautiful world it is."

Chloe falls asleep, because she's exhausted from all the throwing up and crying and thinking nothing is beautiful or nice, not anywhere in the world.

I call Dr. Reynoso.

I have to leave a message with her answering service. I don't expect her to call back, but she does, in less than ten minutes. It confirms something I suspected about her. I had a feeling that she actually cared. But it seemed liked wishful thinking at the time.

She says, "Is everything all right, Jordan?"

I say, "Yes and no." Then I say, "Yes. Pretty much. I think. But Chloe won't be coming in for her appointment tomorrow. She won't be coming back. But you have to trust that she'll be all right. I know this may sound really strange, and I'm beginning to think it's totally insane myself, but I already made up my mind that I just have to try. She wants me to take her to all the really beautiful places like the Grand Canyon and the Painted Desert and Niagara Falls."

Dr. Reynoso says, "That doesn't really sound all that crazy."

"It doesn't?" I was pretty sure it would.

"I don't think so. I guess it depends on what you think it's going to accomplish."

"She wants me to show her that it's a beautiful world." We're both quiet for a minute. It sounded a little crazy. As I listen to the echo of it, sounding crazy, I realize that I've begun to take Dr. Reynoso into my confidence. Which I never do with anyone. Sounds like something that would help, but it's really just the opposite. I like her just enough now to feel mortified if she thinks badly of me. I say, "It's never going to work, is it?"

"Depends on what you mean by 'work.' If you mean will it do her any good, maybe. It certainly isn't going to do her any harm. What we're doing now sure isn't working."

"So you think I should do it?"

"You said you already made up your mind and you have to try."

"Right. I do."

"Okay, I trust your judgment, Jordan."

"You do?" I didn't mean to sound so amazed.

"Of course I do. Just two things I'll ask of you. Call me if you think she's in serious trouble—or if you think you are—and I'll get you a local referral for wherever you are. And also, when the two of you make up your mind whether the world is a beautiful place or not . . . drop me a line and let me know what you decided."

"Actually, we're just trying to convince Chloe."

"Really. You're already positive?"

"Right," I say. "Good point. When we decide, we'll let you know."

I call Otis's sister and tell her that since the house is being sold anyway, we'll be on our way.

I ask her if I can give her a few dollars for Otis's old backpacks and duffel bags.

"Those old things?" she says. "Those dirty, disgusting old things? Take them. You'd be doing me a favor. How people can keep dirty old things like that around I'll never know."

Though I've never bothered to ask, it hits me that she probably wasn't a big fan of Bruno.

I leave a note on the stereo. The kind of note Chloe would write. The kind I know will please her. I say the stereo belonged to a man named Otis, who's dead now. I say he was a little grumpy, but in many ways he was a pretty okay guy. I leave a note on the TV saying it was Chloe's very first one, a present from me, and I'd appreciate it if once a week or so someone watched *I Love Lucy* on it just for old times' sake. I use up all but one sheet of Chloe's drawing pad, but I'm hoping she'll forgive me because I put them to good use.

I flush the rest of the medication down the toilet. It was headed that way anyway.

When Chloe wakes up I say, "I used up all but one sheet of your drawing pad. Do you forgive me for that?"

"Sure, Jordy," she says.

That's when I remember that she forgives me for almost everything. The pills were really the first exception to that rule. Then she looks at the table. Sees that the pills are gone.

"Where did they go?" she asks.

"I sent them away," I tell her. "Because I want you to be happy."

"I want me to be happy, too," she says. I can tell she's a little closer already.

I sit on the edge of the bed with her. "So, tell me, Chlo. Ever been to Niagara Falls?"

"You know I haven't."

"What about the Grand Canyon?"

"Jordy. I haven't been anywhere. You know that."

"The Rocky Mountains?"

"Nope." She's laughing now. Which she hasn't done for as long as I can remember.

"The Painted Desert?"

"I never saw it. Is it really painted? How did it get painted?"

"The Pacific? The Mississippi?"

"I don't even know what those are."

"Would it make you happy to find out? Do you promise not to hurt yourself?"

"No pills with us?"

"Nope. Not a one."

"Then I guess I'd be happier than I am now. And I promise. Yeah."

I'm thinking if we crisscross the country and make our way to the very top of the West Coast, somewhere in Washington state, and cruise down the coast—after we've seen all these other natural wonders, of course—and wind all the way down to Mexico, stopping at every single place along the way, somewhere on that trip will be a place for riding horses on the beach.

I might as well honor that special request. I've never ridden horses on the beach, either, and it certainly sounds beautiful. I tell Chloe the plan.

She says, "Just one thing, though. If we get all the way to the Pacific, and ride horses on the beach, and we've seen all that beautiful stuff, and I still don't think the world is a very nice place, you have to let me go."

"No," I say. "No way. I'm not letting you go."

"That's not fair. You shouldn't make somebody be somewhere they don't want to be."

"But you might change your mind."

"You have the whole trip to change my mind. But if it doesn't, you have to let me go."

"I have to think about this," I say. I really don't think I could stand back and let her go. But I say I agree to the plan. Because it's my last best shot. It feels like the only plan I have left.

I'm just letting everything ride on believing this will work. That we'll find so much beauty and pleasure, and maybe even some decent, kind people, that she'll change her mind about the world. I'm betting everything on thinking I can make her believe it. Even though I'm not positive I believe it myself.

FIVE

OUT IN THE BEAUTIFUL WORLD

We're out on the highway, cruising along at about fifty. The old truck seems to do pretty well at fifty. Anything more and we get a bit of a rattle. The sun is just coming up, glaring into the left side of my face through the driver's-side window.

Chloe is doodling in her new spiral notebook. She asked me to buy her a spiral notebook and a pencil so she could practice writing again. But maybe she's worried about how rusty she really is, because so far she's only drawn pictures.

Just over the border into New York state we stop for coffee and some breakfast. I wonder if Chloe remembers what I told her. Which kinds of foods cost the least money for each meal. It's the food and gas that's going to kill us. There isn't much we can do about the gas.

Chloe stirs seven sugars into her coffee. Her hair looks greasy. We both feel a little dirty and grungy. Because we are.

Because we slept in sleeping bags in the truck bed, and when we stopped at a gas station this morning before dawn to wash up, it was cold, and there was only just so much washing we could bring ourselves to do.

Chloe sets the spiral notebook on the table and flips to a fresh page. She draws a fairly neat, straight line vertically down the center. "How do you spell 'beautiful,' Jordy?"

"B-e-a-u-t-i-f-u-l."

"Really? Are you sure?"

"Positive."

"Okay. If you're sure. I know how to spell 'ugly.' "

Too bad. I would've liked it better the other way around. But I guess she hasn't had much practice on "beautiful." I guess it's one of those things that just never came up.

An hour or two later, driving along the highway, we pass a raccoon lying dead by the side of the road. There's a little trail of blood where he got dragged, and he's puffed up as if he's been lying there for quite a while. Chloe takes out her little notebook and writes. I'm thinking it's too bad that her very first entry can't be in the "beautiful" column.

Then I think, maybe we've passed a dozen beautiful things already, or a hundred. I never thought to notice any, or point them out. Maybe it's my job to do that.

Maybe I'm already falling down on the job.

"Chloe wants to know if she can play with your dog," I say.

They're an older couple, maybe in their fifties, and the dog looks like she needs all the playing she can get. A leggy young Irish setter with energy pouring off her in waves.

"Why, certainly," the wife says. She's a round-faced, overly sweet woman, like she's looked at too many pictures of Mrs. Santa Claus. "Ginger would like that."

I sit down on the bench with them, and Chloe and Ginger have at it.

We're in a park in Buffalo, New York. Why, I'm not sure I can say. We could've driven straight through to Niagara Falls. But no, Chloe wanted to see Buffalo.

Chloe, I said. Nobody wants to see Buffalo.

But Chloe did. And the reason was simple. She'd never seen it before. If Chloe has never seen it before, she wants to see it now. Simple as that. That's what this trip is about, she said. How do we know if it's beautiful if we don't even see it? I felt like Buffalo was a pretty safe "ugly" bet. But it's a nice shift in attitude for her, so I go along.

"She really wants a dog," I tell the older couple. "But we're traveling."

"Well, we're traveling, too," the husband says. He's mostly bald, with just a ring of hair over his ears and a tendency to run one hand over his bare scalp, as if it might not be lying down just right. "Ginger loves to ride in the car."

"Isn't it hard to find lodging that will let you take the dog?"

"Well, sometimes," the wife says. "Sometimes it is hard." She has a girlish voice. High and insubstantial. It makes her sound as if nothing she says could ever hold much gravity. "When we get to Niagara Falls, we'll have to put Ginger in a kennel one night."

"Niagara Falls. That's where we're going. Chloe has never seen Niagara Falls."

"Newlyweds?" the wife asks. Rather hopefully, I think.

"We're just going to see Niagara Falls because Chloe has never seen it. She wants to see new things."

Meanwhile, we watch Chloe and the dog leap around. They both have long hair that flies in smooth waves away from their direction of travel. Ginger has a liking for the play bow, that silly dog thing with the front end down and the back end up, tail going like a hyperactive flag. Chloe seems dead set on learning it. All but the tail part, of course. Though I suppose she'd do that too if she could.

"We go to Niagara Falls every year," the wife says. "We honeymooned there, and now every year we go for our anniversary."

"Happy anniversary," I say.

"Why, thank you," they both say at once. They sound pleased and truly amazed. As if it's a miracle to find someone in a city park who actually cares enough to say those two words.

"I'm Adele," Adele says. "And this is Fred."

We shake hands.

"Jordan," I say. "And that's Chloe. The energetic one."

Chloe is in a state of rapid motion. For a moment I wonder if she has enough energy stored up for this roughhousing stuff. She's barely put on two pounds since the Great Pill Ordeal.

As if reading my mind, Adele says, "She's so thin. Is she always so thin? Has she been sick?"

"Honey," Fred says. "We don't even know them."

"I'm just concerned, Fred."

"It's okay," I say. But I don't know why I say that, because it's really not. "The reason we're traveling is because . . ." Why did I even start with this? Why am I telling them this? Then again, I think, why not? What can it hurt? It's not information that can be used against us. But part of me is like Fred. Honey, we don't even know them. But then there's this other part of me that feels like I'm holding up the whole world in silence, and I just want to set it down for a second, just one second so I can rest. "Chloe's been having some problems. Emotional stuff, mostly. Depression. She doesn't eat much."

"Poor dear," Adele says.

Suddenly I understand why Chloe tells things to people she's never going to see again. It feels good to dump a little bit of that load out loud, and a total stranger seems to make such a good target, because in a minute they'll go away forever and take it all with them.

"Well, it's nice to see Ginger cheer her up," Fred says.

Chloe and Ginger have found a stick now and are growling and wrestling it out in a tug-of-war. Ginger seems to be winning. Ginger is backing up, and Chloe is being pulled forward.

Adele says, "Ginger will sleep like a baby all the way to Niagara Falls. Where are you staying?"

"We're not sure yet. We're camping. Is there a campground that you know of?"

"Oh, yes, there are a couple. But one is much better than the other," Adele says. "Much better location. Make sure you get the good one. We have to make sure they get the good one, Fred. Fred, go get the map and show him how to get to the good one."

While he's gone we sit and watch. Chloe is playing hide-and-seek. Hiding behind a tree. Ginger's tail is going like mad, waiting for Chloe to jump out and chase her. Maybe I really should get Chloe a dog. But it would complicate our situation tremendously. And, also, I hate to deprive her of the joy of playing with everybody else's.

Adele says, "You simply must go on the *Maid of the Mist*. You have to. The trip would be a waste without it."

"Oh. Yeah. That's a great thing. I did that once as a kid. Thing is, we're doing this trip on the cheap. I mean, we have money. We have some savings. But the longer it lasts, the longer we stay out on the road, seeing beautiful things. I really want us to be able to stay out a long time. Because . . . you know . . ." But of course she doesn't. Why would she? "Because I'm not really sure what to expect when it's over. I just know she's okay right now. I don't know how it's going to be when it's over."

Chloe and Ginger are collapsed in the grass now, Chloe with her arms around the dog's neck. Ginger's tongue is hanging crooked out of one side of her mouth, but she looks like she'd go again in a heartbeat if somebody said the word. Adele pats my hand, then wraps her own hand around it and holds on. Her skin feels warm and dry. First I think, How weird is this? Sitting in the park holding hands with a complete stranger. Then I decide that there are a lot of weird things in the world, and this is not the very worst of them.

When we climb in the truck again, Chloe takes out her little notebook and pencil.

"What kind of dog was Ginger again?"

"Irish setter."

"How many t's in setter?"

"Two."

"Irish setters are really pretty."

"I agree."

"And fun."

Maybe I really should get Chloe a dog. When the trip is over.

Depending on what happens when the trip is over. Or maybe we should just stay out here forever, and then everything will always be okay.

We're standing at the railing of the American Falls, and I'm holding Chloe around her waist, just to be on the safe side. Not that she's leaning over dangerously far. But with Chloe, you never know. She likes a real hands-on experience. The roar of the falls fills my ears and head in a pleasant way, driving out unnecessary thoughts. A cool mist settles, wave after wave, on our faces. There's something cleansing about the whole thing. Chloe feels it, too. I can tell.

"What happened to the people who went over in barrels?" she says.

I'm surprised she knows that anybody did. I wonder if she heard a story like that as a kid. Or maybe she overheard something since we arrived here, because she was paying better attention than I was.

"They either all died or most of them did."

"Did anyone live?"

"I'm not sure. I don't remember. I bet we could find out easily enough." I mostly remember this place from my childhood. At the time the barrel thing was not famous as a successful endeavor, but maybe they're making barrels better than they used to. "When I came here as a kid there was a big ship hung up on the rocks. Maybe a few hundred yards back from the falls. It was all rusted out. It's been there a long time. I guess it got stuck on some rocks instead of going over. Talk about luck."

"What happened to the people on it?"

"They got rescued." That's the way I remember it, anyway. I

can't figure out if the boat is gone, long ago rusted away and broken apart by erosion, or if I'm looking in the wrong place.

I want to show Chloe the point of no return, but I can't remember how far upriver it is. I don't think we can walk there from here, but I can't remember. I just remember that I always found it at least as compelling as the falls, if not more so. It's like someone drew a line across the river, and just at that line the water knows to jump into rapids. The kind of rapids you don't row out of. You either miraculously hang up on the rocks or it's over. After that nothing can save you but sheer, dumb luck. Or grace, if you believe in it. Either God throws you a bone or He forsakes you. And I don't know too many instances of boats hanging up on the rocks.

"Maybe tomorrow we can go on the *Maid of the Mist*," I say. I shouldn't say that until I find out how much it costs. But I'm beginning to think there's no point staying out on the road forever if we have to miss the best stuff. "You'd like it. It's a way to see the falls from a boat."

"No way!" Chloe says.

"It's fun, really. I've done it."

"No way am I getting on a boat on that. Who goes on that ride?"

"No, Chloe, not on the river. Down there. Below the falls."

I point, and Chloe looks, and sure enough, there it is. The *Maid of the Mist*, carrying a group of hooded, slickered tourists taking close-up snapshots of Horseshoe Falls.

"Oh, down there," Chloe says. "That could be fun."

"Well, let's wait and see what it costs. Let's not decide until we see."

A policeman wanders by on foot, and Chloe says, a bit too loudly, "I bet he'd know."

He stops walking.

I'm thinking Chloe is going to ask him how much it costs to ride on the *Maid of the Mist*.

Chloe says, "Jordy and I were wondering about all the people who went over the falls in a barrel. Did they all die?"

"No, ma'am," he says. "Quite a few survived. But we definitely don't recommend it."

I half expect Chloe to write that down. In which column, I'm not sure. But I guess she was only asking out of idle curiosity.

When we get to the campground, there's a bored teenager with acne collecting fees in the booth.

"Your name's not Jordan, is it?" he asks.

Chloe says, "Yeah. How did you know? How did he know, Jordy?"

"I don't know."

"This is for you," the kid says, and he hands me an envelope.

"What is this?"

"How should I know? Some people left it here and said to give it to you when you came in. If you came in."

"What people? What kind of people?"

"An old guy and his wife in a station wagon with this really hyper dog in the back."

I open the envelope. Inside are two tickets to ride on the *Maid of the Mist*.

Chloe is looking over my shoulder. "Cool," she says. "If you're sure that ride doesn't start up on the river part."

"Positive," I say. "Trust me on this."

✳ ✳ ✳

We're on the deck of the little boat with rain slickers on. They provide the slickers as part of the deal. The boat is rocking gently under our feet, and the mist is hitting our faces, and it makes Chloe laugh. The hands-on nature of the whole experience just makes her laugh out loud. Fills her with too much joy to contain, and that's what she does to release the balance. She's standing at the rail, and I'm standing behind her with my arms around her waist, just to be double safe.

I get that feeling again. We've seen the falls from the top and now from the bottom, and we've been given a present by relative strangers, and Chloe hasn't written anything new down in her notebook. So I'm still falling down on the job.

I remember her saying—kneeling on the bathroom floor that awful day—maybe you could show me. Maybe she didn't mean just take her to the beautiful places. Maybe she meant show her that they were beautiful. Help her see them through my eyes.

So I plow straight into that theory. "Do you think Niagara Falls is beautiful, Chloe?"

We have to raise our voices to be heard over the falls. Then again, it's harder for anyone else to overhear, so the moment remains private.

"I love it," she says. "It's great."

"Why didn't you write it down?"

"Oh. Right. I forgot. I will when we get off the boat."

"Just Niagara Falls?"

"I guess. What else?"

"Well, Ginger's people gave us a present. And we hardly even knew them. That's a nice thing, right?"

"Oh, yeah. I guess I wasn't thinking about stuff like that. I was thinking about beauty, like, that you can see."

"There are so many other kinds, though. Like you said yourself, Irish setters are not only pretty, they're fun."

"So fun is like another kind of beauty?"

"Yeah, I guess. I mean, it's another good thing. And nice is another one, like when people who hardly know us want to give us a chance to do something fun."

"There's fun again!" she says. "I'll have to write that one down twice."

This is when I realize I really do need to be the tour guide for beauty. It seems weird, because all that time we lived in the worst surroundings Chloe always found the best in everything. Now *I* have to teach *her*. Which is kind of depressing and strange. But then again, if we go all over everywhere and I'm on the lookout for good, I'll find it. Everywhere we go. Now I understand that I get to go places and see things, too.

We glide through New York state at a very slow rate of speed. Not only do we not drive fast, but we make a lot of stops along the way. We try to take the most scenic routes. We stop and roll down the windows and talk to strangers and ask them to tell us the prettiest roads. And they all do, quite happily, because they love where they live and they want people to see the parts they love best. It strikes me that this pride of place is a subtly beautiful thing, but it's a little abstract to explain to Chloe. I'm trying to stick with things she can spell.

While I'm thinking this, a rabbit scurries across the road.

"There," I say. "Look."

"What?"

She doesn't look up in time, and she misses it.

"There was something beautiful, but you missed it. Next time I say 'there,' look real quick, okay? Try to see where I'm pointing."

"Tell me what you saw, Jordy, and I'll write it down anyway."

"A rabbit running across the road."

She takes out her notebook.

I say, "R-a-b-b-i-t."

"I knew that one, Jordy."

"Okay. Sorry." Then, "There. Look." I slow the truck and point to a smoky charcoal-gray cat sitting on the roof of a house.

"Ooh, stop, Jordy, I want to look at that some more."

We sit by the side of the road and the cat watches us back with yellow eyes.

I realize that the more I show her things that are beautiful, the more she'll want to stop and take it all in. And the slower we'll go. But since my secret desire is to never get to the end of the road, I guess I should just keep finding more things. Next I point to a bull scratching his butt on a fence post. Chloe laughs. I laugh. It's really a pretty bizarre sight. Back and forth, up and down. This great, fierce beast looking absolutely preposterous because his butt itches.

We sit there and watch until he's done. It's just too good to miss.

Chloe says, "You really didn't even have to point to that one, Jordy. I could have found that one on my own."

We're headed south. Picking up as southern a route as possible, because we're going to be gradually heading into winter. Because we'll be out here for months, and so will the cold weather. And we're camping, so we need the weather on our side.

Pennsylvania slides by like a pleasant dream, though it takes us nearly ten days to dream it. For some reason we go particularly slowly through Pennsylvania. Must be all the trees.

Then after many fairly uneventful days, we hit a day that's hard. It rains. We want to stop somewhere and get something to eat, but there isn't anywhere. I mean, not on the road we're traveling. Chloe's gotten to really like back roads and scenic routes. More cats and cows and rabbits scurrying across the road. Chloe likes to be the one to ask now. Now she's the one who likes to talk to total strangers. I stop and she asks. "What's the *prettiest* way to go?"

So the road we're on is pretty, but there's no place to stop. No civilization. No services. And the rain is a hard rain. And no cars have passed us. We haven't seen a soul. We've already driven farther than we usually drive at a stretch, and the rain is so hard that there's really nothing outside to see except the rain. And the rain has stopped looking beautiful.

Then I realize we're going up quite a steep grade. So I downshift the gears. I'm using more gas but going slower. I look up and the rain is falling faster than the wipers can sweep it aside, and the grade just keeps getting steeper, and it goes on forever. Miles. As far as my eyes can see, upgrade, with no end in sight. I'm suddenly prone to believing this whole back-road thing was a lousy idea. We should've stayed on the main highway. Because what if the truck won't make it up this grade? Where would we find a call box? How long would it be before some helpful motorist or state trooper happened by? Could be days.

Almost before I finish that thought, the truck engine makes

this god-awful bang. It's like a shot fired. Then I realize that the thought didn't come out of nowhere. I was listening to the engine grind and strain, and the noise it was making was wrong. I just couldn't admit it to myself consciously until after the bang.

The engine dies and we lose momentum almost immediately, and I pull over fast and stop before we start drifting backward downhill. I wrench on the hand brake as hard as I possibly can. Little whisps of smoke are coming up through the grille, and the rain is slicing and twisting them, stopping them from rising. Nearly stopping them from existing at all.

Chloe looks at me and I look at her. Nobody asks the question about what comes next, but it seems to be hanging in the truck anyway. So I turn the key to see if the engine will start. It screams out, that awful metal-on-metal scream, and rattles and bangs, and when I shut it off again, another big puff of smoke comes up from the grille to be dampened down by the rain. I turn the key all the way to off, and it's quiet except for the torrent outside. The windshield wipers have stopped, so the windshield is just a muted sheet of water. It's cold without the heater.

Chloe says, "Maybe somebody'll come by."

"Sure. Sooner or later somebody will."

Only we've been on this road for hours and haven't seen one other motorist. And that was by day. Now the sun is nearly down. We're hungry. We don't have anything to eat or drink.

Chloe says, "So what do we do while we're waiting?"

"Oh. Let's make some more notes in your book."

"Okay." She takes it out and waits with the pencil ready.

"Um . . ." I'm trying to think of something good in all this. I don't want that ugly category getting too big.

"Rain," Chloe says. "Ugly."

"Oh, I don't know. I think the rain is beautiful. It makes the grass grow. There'd be no trees without it. The world wouldn't be green."

"It also keeps us from sleeping out in the truck bed. We can't put our sleeping bags anywhere tonight."

"True."

She writes "rain" in both the "beautiful" and "ugly" columns.

"It's cold," she says. "Cold sucks."

I find that hard to debate.

We have our sleeping bags up front, behind the seats, because we wanted to keep them out of the rain. It isn't easy to pull them free without stepping out of the truck, but we manage. We unzip them and wrap up tight. We don't debate any more columns or categories, but it's hard not to think about it. The sun is almost down. It doesn't seem likely that anyone will come by until morning. Maybe not even then. Maybe in the morning we'll have to get out and hike this monster grade. Maybe even in the rain.

Is a truck good or bad? Is a broken truck good or bad? Should I be grateful for this shelter even though it's not even big enough to sleep lying down? Are there other people who don't even have a tiny dry space and a sleeping bag tonight? And then, the biggest question of all: Even if there are, does that really mean this doesn't suck?

Dear Dr. Reynoso. This is more complicated than I thought. Did you know it would be this complicated? Never mind. Don't answer that.

We fall asleep twisted strangely around each other, half comforted and half disturbed by the drumming of the rain on the roof.

* * *

I wake to a tapping on the window. It's light outside. I'm lying twisted onto my side on the seat, my head in Chloe's lap. When I sit up, I'm in a lot of pain from the cramped position.

It's still raining. There's a man standing in the rain at the driver's-side window.

I roll it halfway down, taking spatters and drops into my hair and eyes.

The man is standing drenched, no hat. No coat, just coveralls. He's missing one front tooth on the top. In my peripheral vision I see his big flatbed truck pulled level with us and parked in the middle of the road. It has a tractor tied down onto the bed. The wind and rain are so loud, or I was sleeping so soundly, I didn't even hear it pull up.

"You folks all right?"

"Not really. We broke down. Can you give us a lift somewhere? Anywhere, really. Just so we're not in the middle of nowhere."

The man smiles broadly, displaying the bare stretch of gums. "Aw, you ain't in the middle of nowhere. There's a town just right over this grade. There's a great little coffee shop and a gas station that does good mechanic work."

"Great, can you drive us there?"

"Well, don't you want your truck to go there, too? Can't do no good mechanic work on a truck if you don't get it there."

"Well, yeah, but—"

"Piece a cake," he says. "You leave it to me."

He swings up onto the back of the flatbed truck. The tractor is tied down with five or six enormous chains. Huge links with big metal hooks on the end that can be hooked back through the

109

chain at any point. The guy frees one, then rearranges the others so the tractor is still secure.

I roll my window up all but an inch or two to keep the rain out of my face, and I watch him through the inch of opening. Now and then a drop still splashes me in the eye. But all and all, I'm dry. The guy on the flatbed is soaked through and through. I'm wondering if I should have offered to help him. Then again, what do I know about tying down a tractor?

I look over at Chloe, who is, amazingly, still asleep. Sitting up, but fast asleep. I stretch and think of how happy she'll be to wake up in a good mechanic's shop. Especially if I can hand her a cup of hot coffee and tell her there's a café with good food nearby.

The guy hooks one end of this gigantic chain somewhere under the front end of our truck, then secures the other end to the towing ball on the back of the flatbed.

He comes back to the window and I roll it down.

"Turn your key to 'accessory' and put your wipers on. You need to be able to see the back of my truck. When we crest the hill, put on your brakes so's you don't roll down and smack me. I'll come back and unhook you. You can coast all the way down into town. The gas station is at the bottom of the hill on the right."

"We really appreciate this," I say.

He smiles another gap-tooth smile. "Ain't no thang," he says.

Then he climbs into the truck and I take off the brake. There's a lurch as the slack comes out of the chain, and then we're rolling. Not fast, but we're rolling.

I turn on my wipers and watch the back of the truck. The tractor is facing me, alarmingly, like traffic going the wrong way in my lane, coming right at me. We must never get beyond first or second gear, because we take the hill at just a few miles an hour.

But, hell, we're going a lot faster than we were without his help.

Then we crest the top of the hill and stop, and he comes out into the rain and takes his chain back. I roll down my window and try to yell "thank you" to the guy but he doesn't seem to hear. I look over at Chloe but she's still fast asleep. The guy waves at me through the rear cab window. I wave back. He pulls away, and we coast. The license plate on the back of his truck says West Virginia, so I wonder if that's where we are already.

We coast at maybe thirty-five, forty miles per hour, rocketing through the rain, and then suddenly there is no rain. Suddenly the air is clear, and one single beam of early sun finds its way out of the heavy clouds and lights a spot on the dark valley below. Farmland. Then I look straight ahead of us, down the road, and there's a town. Services. The kind of town that would have a restaurant and a good mechanic, just like I was told.

I look over to see that Chloe is awake. Somehow the sheer momentum got her attention, even in her sleep. She woke up to feel us going so fast. Past her face I see there's a rainbow stretched across the valley. The sky is still black in that direction; even the air looks black. It's probably still raining over there. But there's a rainbow.

"There, Chloe," I say. And I point. "Right there."

I'm sitting on a tire just outside the service bay, drinking hot coffee. Watching Chloe win over a dog. A skinny little blue-eyed dog with an all-over itch and hardly any hair on its rump and docked tail.

The mechanic, Jim, is leaning into our engine compartment, but he sticks his head out and says, "That dog won't come near you, miss, don't take it personal. She's just shy."

I give Chloe three minutes to win that dog over.

We've had breakfast. I have to admit I feel better. Just getting fed and settled somewhere. Even though I know in my gut that we still have big problems. Unless the problem with the truck is something small and cheap. Thing is, I don't think so. It didn't sound small and cheap. It sounded big and expensive.

The mechanic waves me in. I get up and walk halfway into the service bay, then stop dead when I encounter a sign that says, ABSOLUTELY NO CUSTOMERS ALLOWED IN THE SERVICE AREA.

"Pay that no mind," Jim says.

We lean into the engine together. He's taken something off or apart. I can see engine parts that I know are normally covered. They shine with blackened oil. I try to look at the engine intelligently. As if I will be clear on what I see.

"I'm bad at this," Jim says. "I hate to give bad news. I only like to tell people what I know they want to hear."

"Okay, fine. Tell me what I want to hear."

"Wish I could, dude. Wish I could." Long beat. "Know anything about engines?"

"No."

"Okay. It's like this. The timing chain keeps the cam and the crank running together. That's why it's called a timing chain. Keeps the timing right between the valves and the pistons."

"I thought it kept the timing right between the crank and the cam."

"Right. Camshaft runs your valves. Crankshaft runs your pistons."

"I'm confused."

"Okay, let's go at it another way. You got to have the timing right between your compression stroke and your exhaust stroke, and if you don't . . ." Jim looks at my face and realizes I'm no closer to mastery. "Okay, maybe I'm trying to explain too much. You got serious damage inside this engine. It'll have to be all torn down. Hard to say what we'll find till we open her up. Maybe new pistons and valves and valve stems, and then maybe we'll find out that the cylinder walls are scored and then maybe we can bore and sleeve, or maybe the engine is just trash and you'll have to start all over again with a new short block."

I recognized about three English words in all of that, and they all sounded expensive.

"How much money are we talking?"

"I'm not sure you even want to know."

"What's the very least it could be?"

"Well, we're talking labor and machine work. Even with no nasty surprises I can't see you getting off for less than eleven or twelve hundred."

"Oh."

"More than you can handle?"

"Oh, yeah. Truck's not even worth that. Is it?"

"Hell yeah it is. Are you kidding? '54 Chevy pickup? People kill for these. They restore 'em. Worth a fortune all cherried out. I know two guys within forty miles of here who'd scratch each other's eyes out for this truck. Everything all original. Body in good shape."

"But it doesn't run."

"But these guys, even if it did run, first thing they'd do is haul the engine out and rebuild it. Anyway. I'm not saying that a busted engine brings the price *up* exactly. But lots of people'd still want it."

"What do you think I could get for it?"

Jim scratches his head. "I'd give you eight hundred for it right here right now. But I got to be honest and say you could maybe do better. If I was to give these guys a call . . ." He smiles. Then he smiles even wider, like he'll break into a laugh any minute. "Well, that might be fun to see. These guys don't like each other any too much. One of 'em is just sure the other stole a set of factory original hubcaps off him in the dead of night. If they both knew this truck was for sale, it might just be interesting to see."

We walk out into the light to tell Chloe.

She's sitting on one of the pump islands with the little blue-eyed dog half in her lap. The dog's whole front end is sitting on Chloe's lap, the little stump tail going.

"I'll be damned," Jim says.

They come roaring up at almost exactly the same time. Like they were racing each other in. One is riding on a big, chopped motorcycle. He has a full beard and that kind of helmet that only covers the top of his head. No faceplate or anything. More for looks than safety. The other guy drives a really shiny, sweet-looking red El Camino. He wears a gold wedding ring and has neatly trimmed gray hair. I have a pretty good idea who thinks who stole parts from who.

114

Chloe and I stand off and listen while Jim talks to them in a foreign language. Something about the engine number matching the VIN number, and not a trace of Bondo. I don't know what it means but he makes it sound like a compliment.

I look at Chloe and she looks sad.

"I know, Chlo," I say, "but there really isn't much else we can do."

"Otis would be sad."

"Otis was a practical guy. He'd understand."

"Yeah, but he'd be sad."

"Yeah, okay. We're sad, too. But we have to just do our best here."

"How will we get around?"

"I don't know, but we'll have more money. We can maybe hitchhike sometimes. Maybe we can afford a train or a bus if it's cold."

Just then I hear the motorcycle guy yell, "Bullshit! You know it ain't worth that not running. You know I don't have that. You're just doing it to spite me."

We don't hear any response. A minute later his big bike roars to life and off the lot and down the highway. The guy with the neat gray hair comes and stands over us.

"Son," he says, "I'll give you twenty-four hundred dollars for that truck."

The guy who bought the truck gives us a lift to the main highway so we'll have half a chance hitchhiking. Then a couple named Carlos and Elena stop for us, our first actual ride.

"You've got so much stuff," Carlos says, looking at Otis's old duffel bags and sleeping bags and backpacks. They're young, maybe as young as Chloe and me. They're clean. Inside and out clean. I can't decide if it's scary or nice. "We felt bad for you—you have so much stuff."

"I know," I say. "I'm sorry. Is there room?"

"There's all that," he says, pointing to the bed of his pickup. It's a tan-and-brown truck, not really old like Otis's, but old enough. Maybe from the seventies. It has an extended cab, so Carlos and Elena and their new baby, Maria, and all their luggage—which isn't much—fit up front. "You and your wife and your stuff can fit back there, you're more than welcome to the ride," he says. "Where are you going?"

"As far west as you can take us. Where are *you* going?"

"Lexington," he says. "Home. We were just in West Virginia visiting Elena's parents. We were there to show them our new baby. Their first grandchild."

"A baby," Chloe says. "You have a baby." Her voice is full of wonderment and awe. To Chloe, a baby is nearly as splendid and exciting as an overweight geriatric Doberman pinscher. A close second, anyway.

Elena steps out to let us see the baby, who is sleeping in her arms. She's a very new baby. Maybe a few weeks, tops. Chloe can't stop looking.

Meanwhile, Carlos is throwing our stuff in the back, so I join him and throw stuff, too. "We appreciate this," I say.

"Happy to help," Carlos says. "Boy, that's a nice coat. That's a beautiful coat. That just might be the nicest one I ever saw."

Then we're out on the highway, and Chloe and I are on our backs looking at the sky. It seems like we're racing one way under clouds that seem to race the other way.

Chloe is making notes in her book, but I don't look over her shoulder and I don't ask.

After a couple of hours we stop for lunch.

I'm looking at Carlos, thinking he's attractive. Dark and lean, with a kind face. Reasonably handsome, but more than reasonably attractive. Actually, I'm trying *not* to think that. He's a husband and a father, and anyway, it embarrasses me.

"You should let us help you with the gas money," I say.

They're sitting across the table from us, and the baby is a little fussy. So I'm thinking in a minute Elena will have to go someplace private to breast-feed.

Elena shakes her head no about the money.

"We wouldn't hear of it," Carlos says. "We had to make the trip anyway."

"We can afford to help out a little."

"Come on. Stop it. You guys don't have much."

Elena is beaming at little Maria. Smiling and making faces and cooing and looking down lovingly. And, you know, tiny and new as this baby girl is, I swear she gets it. I swear she's taking every bit of this in.

So is Chloe. She stares all through lunch. Carlos and Elena look up and smile. Then after a while I can see that Elena is not sure about the staring. It seems like too much, even to me. And I know Chloe. I know how intense she can be.

Finally Elena looks to Chloe questioningly. "What?" she asks.

"That's so great," Chloe says. "I never saw anything like it before in my life, but it's great."

"What is?"

"The way you're looking at her. It's so great. She knows, too."

"All mothers look at their babies like this."

"Oh, no they don't," Chloe says. She obviously considers herself an authority. "My mother never looked at me like that. I'm not sure she even looked at me. Then she had six more babies and she never looked at any of them like that, either."

"Oh," Elena says, clearly not sure what to say. "Well, I *wish* all mothers looked at their babies like that."

"You and me both," Chloe says. She turns her attention to me. "What about you, Jordy? Did your mother ever look at you like that?"

"Are you kidding? You met my mother, Chlo."

"Oh. That's right. Never mind."

Carlos wakes me up by shaking my shoulder.

"Sorry, buddy," he says. "Sorry to disturb you. But I need your wife." I open my eyes and see that we're at a rest stop on the side of the highway. "I have to get some sleep," he says. "I'm too tired to drive anymore. I'm going to sleep back here with you. Elena can drive if Chloe will sit up front and hold the baby. Her car seat's broken. Or you can drive if you want."

"I want to hold the baby," Chloe says. She doesn't sound sleepy. Maybe she was never asleep. Maybe only I was asleep.

Next thing I know we're cruising down the road again and Carlos is lying beside me, which makes me happy and uncomfortable in ways I can't quite sort out. I haven't been with many men my own age lately. I'm looking up at the sky, and the stars are out in force. I mean, there are billions of them. I swear, I didn't even know there were so many stars.

I know Carlos is not asleep yet. He's looking at the stars with me.

"It's almost enough to make you believe in God," I say.

"You don't believe in God?"

"Maybe I do," I say. "I'm not sure."

"Elena and I have been born again."

"Oh," I say.

Oh. I hate this moment. I hate it when this happens. I hate to have some warm feeling for someone, a feeling that seems almost wholesome to me, and then suddenly find out that if he could look inside me he'd see something that looks dirty or sick or shameful to him. And then that same nice feeling, I have to try it on through his eyes. Or maybe he would like me anyway. He's a Christian, right? Christians are supposed to be good at that.

Only sometimes they're not.

Dear Dr. Reynoso. It's not always as easy as it was with you.

Chloe is standing beside the truck, saying goodbye to the baby. Little Maria. She's practicing that look. That loving-beaming thing. She still can't get over that look.

Carlos pulls me aside and stuffs a piece of paper in my hand with their phone number.

"If you're ever in Kentucky again," he says, "give us a call."

But I know we won't be. And even if we were, we wouldn't call. If we did, they'd learn more about us and we'd learn more about them. I'd start wanting to sleep with Carlos and they'd start wanting to study the Bible with us.

"Absolutely," I say. "I will. Now please let me give you twenty for gas."

"Nope. Don't even try."

"Hang on a minute," I say. "What size are you? Stand back to back with me for a minute."

He does. Our shoulders seem about the same height and width. So I take off the coat and give it to him.

"You're kidding," he says.

"Please take it, Carlos. I don't even want it anymore."

It's a relief to watch it drive away. I don't realize how much I don't want it until I watch it drive away. I throw away the phone number, just to make sure I never get it back.

The next ride we get is from a lady wearing two big puffy ski parkas. One right over the other, even though it's really not all that cold. But we climb in, because we figure she just chills easily or whatever.

But then I notice that she has about five Fleet enemas sitting on the dashboard. Right in their boxes. She also has three troll dolls pasted to the dash, way over in the corner near the passenger-side window. When I lean forward to get a closer look, I notice she has about twelve more Fleet enemas on the seat beside her. Some are the saline kind and others the mineral oil.

"Don't get too close to the trolls," she says.

I sit back as fast as I can. She tells us that the trolls ward off evil spirits, but as a by-product of cleansing the evil as it comes into the car, the evil gets stuck in the trolls, and if you get too close it can jump into your body and take over.

"Okay," I say. "Good to know. Thanks for the warning."

We ride for about twenty miles in silence. Then she sees a gas station out in the middle of nowhere. "I gotta take a whiz," she says.

We off-load all our stuff while she does. We hide out around behind the station, waiting for her to drive away.

She calls for us a couple times first. "You coming or not?" she yells. "Huh? What's it gonna be?" Then, "Okay. Don't say I didn't warn ya."

"Okay," I say quietly, for only Chloe to hear. "Thanks for the warning."

Chloe and I are standing out on the highway, waiting for a car to go by. So we can stick our thumbs out. We have so much stuff. I didn't realize how much stuff we had until there was no truck to carry it all. Two duffel bags, a backpack, and a sleeping bag each.

We've gotten two good, long rides so far, and all it's gotten us is out in the middle of nowhere again. I'm pretty sure we're still in Kentucky. The air is cool but the sun is hot, and we've been waiting for an hour and haven't seen a single car. Finally we see a van off in the distance. I stick out my thumb and think how awful it will be if this van doesn't stop. What if it's an hour between each car and nobody stops? We're going to have to change this pretty-back-road pattern now that we're hitch-hiking. We're going to have to stay on the big roads.

The van stops for us.

The driver is a guy in his late forties, with the best chest and arm development I think I've ever seen, at least in person. He's wearing a T-shirt, and his biceps are actually stretching out the sleeves. He doesn't get out or even reach over to let us in. He just indicates to us that we should open the side door of the van. We do, and we pile in all our stuff and climb in. There's nothing in the back except three beat-up-looking old bicycles. No seats.

No seats at all except the driver's seat. Not even a passenger seat. Where the passenger seat should be, there's a half-folded wheelchair. I look at the driver again. His legs look like they belong on a ten-year-old.

"Randy Banyan," he says, and thrusts one hand out, which I shake. "Where can I take you folks? First of all, where you been and where you going? If you don't mind my asking. I love hearing where people are going."

"We came all the way from Connecticut," Chloe says. "By way of Niagara Falls."

"That's a strange route."

"Well," I say, "the idea is not to get where we're going fast. More to see the country."

"Seeing the country. Boy. Can't say I don't envy you that. Not that I don't get around. I still speed-race twenty miles every morning after my workout. But cross-country, that's another thing altogether. I may still someday. So, you're headed where?"

"The ocean," Chloe says. "Somewhere we can ride horses on the beach."

"Big Sur, California," Randy says.

"You can ride horses on the beach there?"

"I'm not saying it's the only place, but I know you can. My son just went on a vacation with his wife and my two-year-old grandson, and they sent me pictures of themselves riding horses on the beach at Big Sur. And you know, if you're going to see the ocean, you really ought to see Big Sur, California. One of the prettiest spots on God's earth. Ever been there?"

"No, we never saw that," Chloe says. "And I really like seeing things I've never seen before. Beautiful things."

"Then you definitely have to go to Big Sur."

"We're just not really sure how to get places anymore," Chloe says. "Our truck broke down and we had to sell it."

"Bicycle," Randy says.

"Bicycle?" we both say at once.

"Bicycle," he says. "Can't beat it. Great exercise, cheapest travel there is. Let you see the country in a way you never would zipping through it in a car. I own a bike shop about thirty miles up the road. That's all I do. Bikes. I go all around and pick up old bikes that people throw out. Oh, I sell new bikes and bike parts, too. But I really like fixing up the old ones. It's like bringing something back to life. Sometimes I sell them and sometimes I give them away to the sheriff's department and they give them to kids that can't afford bikes." While he's talking I'm watching him drive and realizing he does it all with his hands. The gas and the brake are both levers he can control with his hands. "If you wanted a couple of bikes, I'd let you have them for just what it costs me to fix them up. Just the cost of the new tires, mostly. Bearings and brake cables and such only cost a couple dollars. It really doesn't cost much to fix up a bike if you know what you're doing."

Chloe says, "I'd like to ride a bike all the way to the Grand Canyon, Jordy."

"I don't know, Chlo. That sounds hard."

"Nah, it's not hard," Randy says. "You're both young, you're in good shape. Ride a little, rest a little. Set a nice easy pace. You said yourself you're in no hurry."

"That's true."

"Come on by the shop, I'll show you what I got. We'll see if it's right for you or not."

*　*　*

The first thing we notice is the cats. The bike shop has a low stone wall out front with two cats sleeping on it. One curled and neat, one sprawled and disorderly. Neither one so much as opens an eye as we lug ourselves and all our earthly belongings by.

Then, once we're inside, I notice there are more cats. Maybe more than a dozen more. And of course Chloe has noticed the cats, too. She's scratching a calico under the chin, and two half-grown gray kittens rise, stretch, and prepare to go investigate Chloe further.

"I like your cats," Chloe says. "How many cats do you have?"

"Lots," Randy says. He wheels in behind us. "More than twenty. Probably less than twenty-five. But give it time. They come and go as they please, so just try to keep count."

Chloe and I pet cats while Randy shows me some good used bikes. I notice he has snug leather gloves with no fingers for handling the wheels of that chair.

"These two here, I'd let them go for fifty bucks for the pair."

"For both?"

"Yeah, I told you, it doesn't cost me hardly anything to fix them up. I don't even buy these bikes, I find them lying around. People give them to me. The frames are always good, they just need a good going over. True the wheels, new tires, brake shoes, brake cables, new bearings all around. They don't look like much but it's just as dependable as a pretty new bike. Maybe not quite as light and fast, but it'll get you there."

"But we have so much stuff."

"I got trailers. Bike trailers, one for each. Won't hold all *that* stuff. But hey, I got some really crappy old saddlebags, too. Look like hell, I could never sell 'em. They're yours. Two trailers, two sets of saddlebags. You could probably take two-thirds of what you've got now."

It's hard to imagine giving up one-third of our meager stuff. Then again, it's hard to imagine walking or hitchhiking with even half of it. Mostly, it's hard to imagine riding a bicycle all the way to the Grand Canyon, or the Pacific Ocean. What about the mountains?

While I'm thinking, Randy is plowing through a storage bin looking for saddlebags. He throws one set over his shoulder into the middle of the shop. Dives in after the others.

"I don't know," I say, "about trying to bike there. I'm worried about those mountains."

Randy's hands stop moving, just for one beat. The look in his eyes changes, like he just left the room. Just for a second, he's looking past everything that Chloe and I can see. Chloe notices, too. She takes her hand off the latest cat. She's watching so intensely. It flashes through my head that I'll look at her notebook later and see she's written "Randy's eyes."

In the good column.

Then Randy speaks, breaking his own reverie slightly. "The mountains," he says. "You're going to the mountains."

"I don't see that we have much choice," I say. "How do you get to the West Coast without going over the Rocky Mountains?"

"Oh, it can be done, if you're willing to dip far enough south, squiggle around a bit. The better question would be, why would you want to?"

"You don't think we're crazy trying to pedal over a mountain?"

"I'd think you were crazy if you had the chance and passed it up. People bike those mountains all the time. They're gentle mountains. There are roads over them. It's not Everest. By the time you get from here to there you'll be in plenty good shape."

A tabby cat brushes against my leg, arching his back. I reach down to scratch him and his tail end rises to meet my hand. "I worry that our timing will be exactly wrong. We don't want to hit the Rocky Mountains in the middle of winter."

"Sure you do," he says. "Of course you do. Afraid of a little cold? Don't be. Just bundle up. Best season of the year in the mountains, the winter. Second best would be the fall. But you'll miss that anyway. Whatever you do, don't go in the spring. Spring in the mountains they call mud season. All the runoff from that melting snow. Half the time the roads are impassable and the rest of the time they're just a mess. And you don't want to go in the summer because of the thunderstorms. No, you'll be up there at a great time. You won't be sorry. Where're you thinking of crossing over?"

"We're not sure," I say. "Maybe you can suggest something. You seem to know the mountains pretty well."

Randy is putting a trailer and saddlebags on one of the bikes now. He turns the chair around, and before he can wheel it back to his tool kit, a black cat jumps up onto his lap and takes the ride with him.

It occurs to me that I haven't exactly said yes yet, but it's all just happening anyway.

"There's not a mountain over twelve thousand feet in the contiguous United States I haven't stood on top of. I'm proud to say."

"So where do you think we should go?"

"Straight," he says. "You're in a hurry to get up there before the thaw, so go straight. Don't bother going north into Colorado like everybody always does. Can if you want, but it'll only set back your time. They got Rocky Mountains in New Mexico, too, you know. The Sangre de Cristo range. And if you go due west from here, maybe bow just a little bit south, like you're headed for Big Sur, you'll find out yourself how pretty they are. You'll end up around the Taos and Santa Fe area. If you get a chance, stop in a pretty little town called Angel Fire. I spent a month there once. One winter."

I'm pretty sure Chloe is off in her own world, which is a cat world. She has seven of them now, all clustered around her, sniffing and rubbing against her and purring. But when she hears about Angel Fire, she comes back to us. "Angel Fire," she says. It's like she's rolling the words around in her head and then testing them out. "I can't believe there's a place called Angel Fire."

"It's a ski resort town," he says. "A little commercial in the winter. A little busy. But it's right next door to the Carson National Forest. Now that's the mountains. That's undeveloped wilderness. You want to climb a mountain, climb Wheeler Peak. Highest peak in New Mexico. Once you're in Angel Fire, it's the mountain next door."

"Jordy, we have to go there," Chloe says. "I want to go to Angel Fire."

"Ever been to the mountains?" Randy asks Chloe.

"No, never," she says. "And I really like seeing things I've never seen before."

"You'll love it up there," he says. "I know you will. You're a mountain person. I can see it in your eyes. You'll get up there and you'll never want to leave again."

That look crosses his eyes again. We both catch it.

When he's all done with the bikes he charges us a grand total of seventy-five dollars for the whole deal. I feel a little disap-
pointed, because now we have to go.

"I guess we're going to have to stop and buy a lot of cold-
weather gear."

"Army surplus store right on your way out of town," he says.
"Other end of this street, on the right-hand side. Unless you
want to get a bunch of that stuff for free."

That just sits in the air for a moment, and I'm not quite sure
what to do with it.

"In return for what?" I ask.

"Well, it's pretty simple," he says. "You'd just have to climb a
mountain for me."

Randy takes us back into his house, which is right behind the
shop. Through a garden area that's beautiful even in the fall.
Rocks formed into planting beds, a marble fountain, and bare
trees.

In the house are more cats.

Randy wheels himself to a closet, throws it open, wheels inside. Winter jackets fly out over his head. "People give me this
stuff because they know I'll give it away again. To just the ones
that could use it, you know? It doesn't all look too pretty. Kind
of ratty and old, but the point is to be warm, right?"

"Right," we both say.

"Now, you say you got good sleeping bags."

"Yeah, we needed that just to get this far."

"What about a tent?"

"We don't have a tent."

"What about socks?" he asks. "Socks are very important.

People all the time go out in the cold and snow and forget decent socks."

"Well, we have socks," Chloe says.

"But not wool ones."

"No," I say. "Not wool ones."

"Here," he says. "Here's a whole box of wool ones. Take about four pairs each. Now all of this has been washed, so don't feel weird about who was wearing it last. Ski masks. One for each of you. Make all the difference. Keep your ears and nose from freezing. Also keep all your body heat from going out the top of your head. And gloves. Here are a whole bunch of gloves. Find two jackets that fit you, I think we'll have it. Oh. Have you got pads to go under those sleeping bags? I didn't think so. Take two pads, keep the cold from coming right up through the bag from the cold ground."

"We've never climbed a mountain," I say. "I'm not sure we'd even know how. Not to mention climbing one for somebody else."

"Wheeler is a gentle mountain," Randy says. "It's nontechnical. There's a trail all the way up. It's just a day hike. I'll give you two pieces of advice and you'll be fine. First off, don't try to get at the mountain as the crow flies. There're good trails and bad trails. Go in at the trailhead at the Taos Ski Valley. When you look at the map you'll think I'm crazy, taking you around in a circle like that. But trust me. Set up camp there by the trailhead. Like a base camp. Get a good night's sleep. Or even two. Longer you spend up there, the more you'll acclimate to the altitude. Then climb the mountain first thing in the morning. You're climbing to a little over thirteen thousand feet. The air is thin up there. So you'll want plenty of time to adjust.

Secondly, stop at the ranger station and get more advice. Tell them you never did this before. They'll give you a trail map and show you the best trail, and tell you what you'll need and what to watch out for. There's people up there that know the mountain. Never be afraid to ask questions. Never guess what you could ask." He digs even farther into the back of the closet. "One more thing you need that you probably don't know you need. But you do."

He pulls out two pairs of what look like snowshoes. Not that I've ever seen snowshoes.

"Snowshoes?"

"Yup."

"We'll need those?"

"You might. Of course, it's been a mild winter. Not much snow in the mountains. So maybe it's patchy and you can work around it. Then again, which is worse, having what you don't need or needing what you don't have? Now you folks dig around and get what you need. I'm going to go make us some lunch. You're going to climb a mountain for me, we have to break bread together."

Randy makes us tuna sandwiches.

Chloe says, "Oh, good. I like tuna sandwiches."

There's also sweet coleslaw with carrots and raisins, and Chloe likes that, too.

We're eating outside in the garden. Drinking a cold root beer with our lunch. The weather is slightly cool, and I can feel the nip in the air fill my head and my lungs, but I don't mind. In fact, I'm beginning to like it. I'm beginning to think even the mountains will be okay. And that was my last big reservation about this trip. I watch it fly away and I feel light without it. I feel free. I'd like to see a place called Angel Fire, too.

"Here's the deal," Randy says. "You walk out of here with all that stuff. Everything you need to camp in the mountains. And all you have to do is climb up to the summit of Wheeler Peak and stick this in the ground."

He sets his plate on the patio floor, and a white cat with gold eyes sniffs at his tuna. Licks the edge of the sandwich. Randy wheels over to the porch of his shop and comes back with something in his lap. Something small and wooden and T-shaped. He hands it to me.

I take it in my hands and look at it. It's a wood sign, about eight inches by six inches, on a two-foot-long stake that's been tapered to a sharp point at the end. The sign itself is hand carved, with raised wings like angel wings and a decorative border. Above the wings, etched in with a wood-burning tool, are the words RANDY BANYAN WAS HERE. Then, on the wings themselves, it says, IN SPIRIT.

"Just climb up to the summit and stick this in the ground?"

"Preferably with the right spirit. You can do it like a chore if you want. I can't really stop you. But I'd prefer you do it like it means something."

"It does mean something," Chloe says. She takes it from me. Holds it on her lap, reading the words as if in Braille.

I can tell that Randy feels better now that she's holding it. Chloe is the one he trusts to do this. It makes me feel bad, just a little bit. But I also feel that, somewhere between here and the summit, I can become the kind of person he trusts to do this thing right.

"What I'm about to say may sound kind of silly," he says.

"It won't," Chloe says.

They're on the same page now, talking soul to soul. I'm the eavesdropper, trying to catch up. But I will. I have time left. I can catch up.

"When you get up there . . . look out over the mountains with my eyes. Think about me. Think about my face and try to feel what I'd feel if I was on that mountain myself."

"Joy," Chloe says.

"Right," Randy says. "Exactly."

Then he turns to me. As if knowing I could begin to feel left out in a moment.

"What I'd like you to do," he says, "is take some pictures and send them back to me. A picture of you guys on the summit holding the sign, or the sign in the ground on the summit. Whatever makes a nice picture."

Then he wheels back into the house.

I finish my tuna sandwich. Chloe feeds the rest of hers to a fat cat.

"I'm not stupid," we hear Randy say. So we know he's on his way back out again. "I know you can take all this free stuff and not do anything I just asked. You could lose the sign or forget to take a camera onto the mountain with you." He's back outside now, with a photo album on his lap. "Hell, you could throw that sign away as soon as you get clear of my shop. Funny thing, though. Turns out nobody ever does."

He hands me the album. Inside are photos of groups of people in cold-weather gear. Some are couples, some groups of young guys. All are standing on the tops of mountains with spectacular views all around and behind them. And all are holding wooden signs announcing that Randy Banyan was there with them in spirit. Chloe takes the album from me. Holds it in her lap and looks at the pictures. Touches the pictures.

"Wow. The mountains are so beautiful."

"Closest thing to heaven in the world," Randy says. "The higher up you get, the closer you are to heaven." He has that look again. That faraway cast to his eyes.

Chloe looks right into that faraway cast, and I think for a second that maybe she's gone elsewhere, too. "Your spirit will be really happy up there," she says.

"I'm sure it will," Randy says. "It always was before."

Then he has to go break up a cat fight up front in the shop.

Over the next couple of weeks, Chloe and I bike. We bike slowly, first just ten miles at a time, twice a day. Then we pick up the pace. We had to weed our stuff down a lot. After we took on all that cold-weather gear, we had to ditch half of what we left home with. Mostly clothes. Every second or third day we stop at a coin-operated Laundromat and do a load of wash. You really only need a couple of changes of clothes to get by.

I've gotten in the habit of pointing at things. Good things. Later, when we stop for water or a meal, Chloe writes it all down.

Randy was right. You see things you might otherwise miss.

I point to a squirrel running across the road. I point to a cat in a high crook of a tree near dawn. A horse leaning over a fence to try to reach an apple on a tree in the pasture next door.

I point to kids. Riding in the backs of pickup trucks, playing softball in vacant lots. Running for the ice cream truck. We wave to them, and they almost always wave back. I point to a stream that runs along the road, spilling over rocks. A gnarled old tree hung with moss, sitting alone in a field all by itself. I point to people laboring in a field, picking crops. What kind of crops, we can't tell from the distance. Something green and about waist high. The weather has taken a turn, into a hot Indian summer, and it looks like hot work, and I'm thinking maybe I shouldn't have pointed. I won't be able to defend myself if she asks where the joy is supposed to be hiding.

"But, Jordy," she says, "that's such hard work."

"Hard work can be joy."

"Yeah, right. If you're not doing it."

Then we crest a good-sized hill, but I'm not too winded now because I'm getting in shape again. Because I've been riding, so now I can do it. So maybe it's true. Maybe hard work can be joy. If you can do it, maybe there's joy in knowing you can. I'm not trying to say that those people picking crops felt any joy at all. But maybe I just meant *our* joy. Our joy at getting to see food growing. After all, it's our joy we're after. Not really anybody else's. I think everyone has to find their own. Unless they have me to help point.

We wave at everybody we see. Cars going by. People walking down the road, sitting on porch swings, mowing their lawns. Kids on bicycles of their own. When we go through a town, this keeps us pretty busy. Then we get out onto the back roads again and we have a chance to rest our arms. Every time somebody waves back, which is often, I say, "There. Right there." And of course she can't argue. Total strangers saying hello. If that's not it, where is it? If you can't see it there, you're not trying.

Then one day we wave at some teenagers in a van and they give us the finger.

Chloe says, "Well, there's one more for the 'ugly' column."

"I don't think so, Chloe. I think you should put it on the good side."

"I think you've been in the sun too long, Jordy. What could possibly be good about getting flipped off?"

"Because it almost never happens," I say.

"Okay, I'll tell you what," she says. "I'll put it on the 'ugly' side, but under 'beautiful' I'll put that it almost never happens."

"Okay. I can live with that."

I point to a red dog who chases our bikes, growling and nipping at our heels.

"But, Jordy," she says. "He's trying to chase us off his street."

"I know," I say. "But aren't you still kind of glad we got to see it?"

She's beginning to question who's the joy expert of this adventure. Still, if I say I see it, who is she to say it's not there? Besides, while she's arguing with me about it, she's only missing something else good.

So she mostly just writes it all down.

We get our first good look at the Mississippi.

Chloe says, "Whoa. That's a big river."

"It's the Mississippi, Chlo."

"Yeah? So?"

"The Mississippi is a big river."

"I know. That's what I just said."

We stop our bikes and just stand and take it in for a moment.

I never really thought much about the Mississippi. Never thought of it as something I just had to see. But I'm kind of blown away by it now, just the sheer size of it, the width and the mass of water, and the pull of it. There's something grand and powerful about the whole thing.

Chloe says, "Where does all the water go?"

"It dumps out into the Gulf of Mexico."

"Well, then how does it stay full?"

First I think it's a silly, childlike question, but as I try to answer it I realize it is kind of mind-boggling. Sure, in my head I know that water evaporates and then it rains and water flows down from the hills in small tributaries and feeds the river again, and yet . . . Looking at that sheer mass of water, knowing it's racing to dump into the gulf, it's really hard to imagine the process that could keep it so consistently full. That's just so damn much water to be constantly replacing. I guess it's one of those things you have to see to believe.

Just as I'm adjusting to that one, she says, "Why does it flow that way? Why not the other way?"

I guess it's something about finding the ocean and I guess it starts with elevation and gravity, but as I go to explain I discover I'm really not qualified because I really don't know. There's so much I see every day and don't really understand and I just don't stop to think about the fact that I don't really understand.

"It's really beautiful," Chloe says.

"Yeah," I say. "It is."

We stand on our bikes and stare at the river a moment longer, and I'm struck by something strong and sudden. A sort of appreciation for getting to do all this. I set off to do it like a sacrifice I'd make to improve Chloe's situation, but as a result I get to see all these amazing things I never would have seen otherwise, and I feel lucky.

I flash back to the time in New York, just before Chloe came barging through the window and altered the course of everything. Where was I headed? I know I was not headed here. That's all I know for sure. Not here.

Somewhere in the middle of rural Arkansas she points to a forty-ish black couple sitting on the porch of a modest red ranch house, fanning themselves, smiling and waving to us as we go by. This time the other people waved first. This time Chloe pointed.

"There," Chloe says. "Right there."

"Don't you get hot?" the woman calls out. She has a round, meaty face. Thick eyelids. A face that's seen a thing or two. "Don't you get hot and tired riding?"

We stop, because if we don't stop, we'll blow right by them before we've had a chance to answer. "Yeah, sometimes we do," Chloe calls.

Lately the onset of winter has been the least of our concerns. Instead we're stuck in this late Indian summer. The temperature in this part of Arkansas today is eighty degrees in the shade.

"Why don't you come sit on the porch with us and drink some cold lemonade?" the husband asks. He has big pork-chop sideburns, going gray. A smile that would warm you up on a cold day, which I'm beginning to wish for. "Tell us where you're going and where you been."

"See?" Chloe says. "I told you to look right there."

After we've each had two glasses of lemonade, paid for with stories from our travels, Mrs. Dodd asks if we wouldn't like to go for a cool swim.

"You guys have a pool?" Chloe asks.

Our hosts both laugh. "You're from the city, aren't you?" Mr. Dodd says. "I bet you never swam in a real-life swimming hole."

"No, sir," Chloe says. "I never have. And I really like doing things I've never done before."

"Go get Trent," Mrs. Dodd tells her husband. "I think he's down by the barn."

"I'm right here," a new voice says.

We turn to look, and I see a teenager, maybe sixteen years old, in jeans and a sleeveless white T-shirt. He's been standing twenty paces from the porch on the barn side. Watching us, I guess. For how long, I don't know. He's dark-skinned, with hair loosely cropped and a little uneven. Muscular, in a thin, wiry sort of way. He looks shy.

"Trent," Mrs. Dodd says. "These nice young folks are on the road traveling. They're hot and they're tired. They come all the way from Kentucky on those bicycles over there. We put some cold lemonade in 'em, but now it's your turn. Bring Bailey and Margie around. They can ride Margie double. You take 'em out and show 'em your swimming hole. Then when you all get back I'll have some nice dinner made."

"We should probably get on the road before dinner," I say. "It's a very nice offer, but if we're going to get settled in by dark—"

"You'll be settled in by dark," she says. "You bet you will. In a nice clean stall in our barn with lots of extra straw. You start pedaling again first thing in the morning. Before the sun gets quite so mean as she's been."

Chloe says, "Who's Margie?"

"She's a big old swayback nag," Mr. Dodd says.

I look up to see Trent walking back to the barn, as instructed, to bring them around. Chloe looks to me for clarification.

"A horse," I say. "Margie is a horse."

"We get to ride a horse? I never rode a horse before. We're going all the way to Big Sur to ride horses on the beach. This'll be good practice, huh, Jordy?"

"Margie is a good old girl for a new rider," Mr. Dodd says. "That old mare is so sweet she won't even swat her own flies."

Trent brings them out of the barn barebacked, in just bridles, the reins hanging slack in his hand as the horses amble along behind him. I realize I'm a little nervous to go off alone with Trent, because he's so shy. Because his awkwardness makes me feel awkward.

"Wow," Chloe says. "I get to ride a horse. I never got to ride a horse before. Aren't you glad I saw this place, Jordy? Aren't you glad I pointed here?"

She runs to meet the horses halfway, and I follow her.

"Trent!" Mrs. Dodd calls out. "You keep your underwears on. None of that skinny-dipping like you do with your family. These folks are not your family."

We're standing on the bank of the watering hole, and I'm unbuttoning my shirt. Trent is down to his boxer shorts already. He still hasn't said so much as a word to us. The horses are grazing at the scrubby grass behind us, their reins trailing on the ground, a signal to stay close by and wait.

Chloe takes off her jeans. She's wearing her red panties today. She pulls her shirt off over her head. She's not wearing a bra.

Chloe never wears a bra. She hates the feel of one, and besides, she doesn't really need to. Her breasts aren't really that big.

I find myself uncomfortable suddenly, and wondering if this was a good idea. Trent is a stranger, and he's also a sixteen-year-old boy. I'm not sure how comfortable I am with a sixteen-year-old boy staring at Chloe's breasts. Except for one thing. He's not. He hasn't even glanced at Chloe's body. He's pretending to look at the ground, but from the corner of his eye he's actually watching me take off my jeans.

Chloe shrieks once with pleasure, holds her nose, and leaps into the water. When she bobs up again, she shrieks even louder. Pushes wet hair off her face. Then she swims away. When did Chloe learn to swim? I wonder. She must have had a real life at some point, and I suddenly hate knowing so little about it.

Trent opens his mouth for the first time and it startles me. "Swimming in your underwears is nasty. Then they're still wet when you get dressed. And then your jeans get all wet."

We look each other in the eye for the first time. Then he averts his gaze. We both step out of our shorts and stand naked at the edge of the water, ready to jump. In this one simple moment I not only know who he is and where he's coming from, but I know I've been busted. I may be traveling with a woman, but Trent looked right through all that. That's how naked I am, standing here with this stranger. I jump in and we swim.

Trent has a big brother, Bart, who rides in from a far pasture to have dinner with us.

We all hold hands and say grace. I'm holding hands with Chloe and Bart. Trent is across the table from me. I look up and catch his eye, and he looks away again.

We eat homemade chili ladled over split cornbread. We drink sweet iced tea. I can't remember when I was ever hungrier. I can't remember food ever tasting any better than this.

Every time I look up at Trent, he's looking at me. But every time I catch him looking, his eyes dart away again.

"I really want to thank you folks for all this hospitality," I say.

"We got more than enough to go around," Mrs. Dodd says. "You're more than welcome to what we got."

I want to say that this was a great day for Chloe. Riding a real horse and swimming in a swimming hole in her underwear. Two very important things she never did before. But how could they understand, really? How can they know how important these little things are to Chloe? How much of a difference they could make to her situation in the long run?

After dinner Chloe asks if she can help with the dishes.

"You *want* to help with the dishes?" Mrs. Dodd asks.

"Yeah. It would be fun."

"Girl, you are my kind of company," she says. "Trent, you go out and get a pitchfork and get our guest room all made up and ready."

I follow Trent out to the barn in the dark, carrying our blankets under my arm. Trent has a flashlight, and I watch the beam of it slide across the dry grass.

There's no electricity in the barn. Apparently not. He sets the flashlight on the ground still lit like a weak lantern. He brushes by me to get the pitchfork, purposely bumping up against me on the way by.

I'm thinking maybe I should go back to the house. But I don't. I stand behind him, watching him fork straw into a clean stall. I feel as though he can feel me watching. And I can hear him feeling me watch. It's enough electricity to make me worry for all that dry tinder.

I hear Bailey making contented little horse noises in the next stall.

When Trent's done, he turns around and looks at me.

"All done," he says. And we stand face to face for an awkward moment.

I'm not going to pretend the thought doesn't cross my mind.

I put all my sexual stuff on hold a long time ago. Told it to sit down and shut up and await further instructions. And it's worked pretty well. But now I can feel it down there, wanting to know how long it's supposed to wait. It talks to me, sensing this opportunity. It says, Let me out, just this one night, and then I'll go back in and be good again. But that's a lie.

Sex urges lie, all the time. They'd tell you any kind of shit to get their way. This is the biggest lie of all. If you let it out for one night, it doesn't go right back in the box again. It grows big and strong and then it won't even fit. Then it laughs at the box and laughs at you, and says, How did you think you were going to keep me in there? And it's too late, because you let it out. Mine tries one last mean trick on me. Brands me with an image of Trent falling to his knees in the straw. He would do it, it says. You know he wants to. You know you want him to. Before I can successfully wrestle that one away, Trent lurches forward and tries to kiss me. I just barely feel his lips touch mine, and then my head jerks back and the connection is broken again.

"Whoa," I say. "Whoa."

He turns around and sits down in the straw with his back to me.

"Did I just do a really stupid thing?" he asks. His voice is thin and small, like I just made him younger. "Did I just make a complete jerk of myself? I thought—"

"You thought right," I say. "You're right. But I can't. I just . . . I don't know how to explain it." I just don't see where the joy is in that. Not anymore. Having sex with a total stranger and then moving on the following day. I just don't understand the joy in that. And there's another thing. It's easier to say, so I do. "I'm a guest in your parents' home. I don't think that's the way they were hoping a guest would behave."

I sit down next to him, but he still won't look at me.

Trent says, "Is it about her, too?"

"Well, maybe a little. I mean, we don't have sex. But we're a team. We do everything together right now. I'd hate to do anything to break that apart. For now, I mean."

"Why you don't have sex if you're together like that?"

"It's just not like that with us."

"Why then? Why you even with her?"

"It's not always about sex, Trent. Everything isn't always about sex. Some people are just together. Sometimes they just are."

Chloe and I are lying on the thick straw bed together. Chloe is comfortably draped over my chest. Trent is sitting at the end of the stall with his back up against the half-door. The flashlight is off. We're just sitting here together in the dark. Talking. It turns out Trent talks. Who knew?

"I hate being a virgin," he says.

"I don't blame you," Chloe says. "You should always try everything at least once."

Then a silence falls, but a comfortable one.

It's funny, because just an hour ago I was stinging over the strange newness of this whole thing. The way it banged into my life like a speeding car might crash through a picnic, leaving me half shocked and more than a little bit invaded. Now we're sitting alone together in the dark, all three of us, and Trent has been holding forth on all kinds of life topics, and I think back to my morning, and it seems strange because there was no Trent anywhere on the horizon, and I didn't know to expect one. Life keeps changing so quickly. I wonder which column that belongs in.

"Don't be in any hurry," I tell Trent. "I know that's easy for me to say."

"I think sometimes about moving to San Francisco. I think it would be better there. But all my family is here. I got to at least finish high school."

"Are you going to college?" I ask.

"Not sure yet."

"You should go to college. It'd be a half step between Arkansas and San Francisco."

"Think I'd meet somebody there?"

"Wouldn't be surprised."

"My grades are good enough. My folks want me to go. They don't even know, by the way. So do me a favor and don't say nothing. Not that I think they wouldn't love me anymore. I'm their son and all. I'd still be their son, right? I'm just trying to find the right way. How did you tell your folks?"

"They pretty much stumbled on the information themselves."

"And were you still their son?"

"No. But then, I never really had been. You're right, a thing

144

like that can't change everything. You're either their son or you're not."

"What are you guys doing going all around the country like this?"

"Jordy is showing me all the beautiful stuff," Chloe says. "All the stuff I've never seen. He thinks the world is beautiful. So he's showing me."

"It is," Trent says. "I never been more then sixty miles outside where we are right now, and I can tell you for a fact the world is okay."

"You sure, Trent?" Chloe asks. Like she'll really believe him if he stands by the opinion.

"Sure as I can be."

We hear a different voice suddenly, and it makes us jump. "Trent!" it says. It's his mother. "Get on in the house and let these poor tired souls get a decent night's sleep."

"Good night, Trent," Chloe says. "Sorry you have to go."

In the morning Trent brings us half a loaf of home-baked wheat bread and a bottle of milk. Breakfast for the road. His father is already out working in the field and his mother has already driven into town, but they said to say goodbye and have a great trip. Chloe kisses everybody goodbye. Sincere kisses on the face, with hugs to follow. First Bailey, then Margie, then Trent.

"Your parents will always love you," she tells Trent. "You're their son."

On the one hand, she's absolutely right. On the other hand, it never worked for either one of us, so I wonder how she's able to know.

* * *

Chloe and I are cycling in the dark on a quiet road. I'm guessing it's about nine o'clock at night. We see a glow in a field up ahead. See it light up the sky. A kind of reddish glow illuminating the night. It makes the trees look spooky.

She says, "I wonder what that is, Jordy."

Then we hear a siren coming up on us from behind. We stop the bikes and walk them off the road, just to be safe. A fire engine roars by, its lights flashing around and around.

We walk our bikes up around the bend until we see three more fire trucks. We lean the bikes on a tree and go a little closer on foot. Right up to a rail fence, where we lean over and watch the farmhouse burning down. It's completely engulfed, with flames curling out the windows and columns of smoke twisting up to the sky. Firefighters are training three or four big arcs of water onto the house at once. The window frames and porch supports are all blackened and cracked, shiny black charcoal. Just as I'm thinking that, the porch awning collapses, throwing smoke and ash in the direction of the firefighters. It's hard to stop watching.

Then a big piece of the roof collapses, raising a shower of sparks that fly hundreds of feet. It sparks a big handful of grass fires, which the firefighters have to try to put out at the same time.

It dawns on me that if the dry grass gets going, this is a bad place to be. So I grab Chloe by the arm and try to pull her away. She doesn't really get pulled, though. She's holding on to the fence. And the fire is holding on to her. Finally an arm of the brushfire races toward the fence, and I grab her hand and pull and she runs with me, back to the bikes.

We ride a mile or two down the road, Chloe looking back

over her shoulder every second or two. Then we see a diner that looks open. There are people inside. It seems too good to be true, in such backcountry. A diner open at nearly ten o'clock.

We lock up the bikes and stick our heads through the door. "You open?"

There's just a waitress inside, leaning on the counter drinking coffee, and a heavy old man back in the kitchen, staring out from under the warming light into the empty dining room.

"Yeah, I guess, hon," the waitress says. "Might as well come on in if you're hungry. Usually we close at nine, but we're staying open tonight for the firefighters. They might be coming by all hungry and thirsty any time now."

We sit at the counter and order grilled cheese sandwiches and French fries.

"Whose house is that?" Chloe asks.

"Oh, a family name of Pete and Dorothy Rogers and their kids."

"They're not still in there, are they?" I ask.

"Oh, no, hon. I hear everybody got out fine."

Then we don't know what else to say to them, or them to us, because we don't know each other at all, and it isn't even us they're staying open for.

We just eat quietly for a while, except when Chloe says, "These are the best French fries."

"Thank you," the guy in the kitchen says. He hardly sounds like he bothers to wake up to say it.

The waitress comes out from behind the counter and wipes off a bunch of tables that I really don't think needed wiping. She's wearing white stockings, and her varicose veins make a strange pattern underneath. Every now and then she goes to the front window and peers down the road. I don't get the impression that she sees what she wants to see. Whatever that is.

Then the first fire truck pulls up and about seven firefighters pile in, their big waterproof jumpsuits peeled down to the waist, their hair plastered to their heads with sweat. Their hip boots make a strange sound as they mill about the place.

They almost all just want coffee to go. One wants coffee and a Danish.

When they pick it up at the register they try to settle up, but the waitress holds up her hands like two stop signs. "No charge, guys."

One of the guys tries shaking money at her, pushing it at her, but nothing works.

"Okay, thanks, Dori," he says.

Dori says, "What those poor people are gonna do, I don't know."

"They got family, though. They got family enough to take 'em in."

"I guess, yeah." She makes a kind of tsking sound with her tongue, like the whole thing is just too tragic for words.

Then the guys all pile out again, and Chloe and I get back on the road.

We ride all night, without ever opening our mouths to discuss the plan with each other. We just keep riding. We really don't say another word all night.

In the morning we set up our tent in the middle of nowhere, hoping this middle of nowhere doesn't belong to anybody who'll tell us to go. Chloe takes out her notebook and writes. But I notice that she's writing on a page that's not divided into columns. Also that she doesn't stop as soon as she usually does. She fills up about two pages. I'd like to know with what, but it's like reading someone else's diary, I guess. Maybe someday she'll show me her notebook from the trip. I'd be interested. But it has to be her own idea.

Chloe has more of a sense of direction and timing now. She wants those damn mountains. Her inner eye is on them, and she won't let go.

She even takes the lead when we ride now, like that will put her closer.

When we stop for a meal or to rest, she says, "Are you sure this is the road to Angel Fire?"

"Absolutely," I say. "Route 64. Goes within a few miles of it. Through Agua Fria."

Sometimes I show her the map so she can see for the tenth time or the twelfth time that Route 64 still intersects with the road into Angel Fire, just like it did yesterday.

Today she looks at the map all through lunch, when she should be eating.

"You have to eat something," I say. We're fairly fresh over the border into New Mexico, and the mountains are coming, and Chloe's getting excited. And when Chloe gets excited she doesn't want to eat. "You know how high Angel Fire is?" I ask, to try to hammer home a point about the food issue.

"Not as high as heaven."

"No. Not that high."

"Not as high as Wheeler Peak."

"No. But it's eight thousand feet. The town. The ski resort is higher. It's not easy pedaling to eight thousand feet. You need to keep up your strength."

"I'm not hungry."

"If you plan on getting to Angel Fire, you have to eat. That's a fact of nature."

She puts down the map, picks up half of her B.L.T. Eats about five bites in rapid succession, barely stopping to chew. "There," she says, her mouth still full. "Are you happy?"

When we get our first glimpse of the Sangre de Cristos, Chloe just stops. Not just stops pedaling. Puts on the brakes and stops her bike and we just stand there at the side of the road and look. We can see the tree line. See the snow on their peaks, settled into the folds and crannies. Patchy, like Randy said. "I feel better already," she says.

When we get close enough to see Angel Fire, Chloe's whole mood changes. Her whole physical bearing changes. She sits up straight and she's pedaling hard and fast, ready to get to someplace that I expect she sees as almost home. At least a solid destination. We stop the bikes to look.

The day is lightly overcast, making the sky look white, with the shaggy green of the pine trees as a friendly contrast. We watch our breath puff out in clouds. The air is thin up here, making me breathe a lot more and a lot harder. I feel like I'm gasping for breath all the time. But it's okay. It's okay to go heavy on breathing. It reminds you you're alive.

"Randy was right," Chloe says. "When you're closer to heaven, you can just tell. You can just feel it. I bet when I think about Randy he can tell. I bet he's back in his bike shop right now and when I think about him I bet he gets that look in his eyes." Then she points in the direction of the ski lifts. "What are those?"

"They take skiers up the hill again. So they don't have to walk back up every time."

"Maybe we should ride one, just to see what it's like to fly like that," Chloe says.

We're settled into our motel room for the night, and Chloe takes off all her clothes because she's going to take a hot bath. We've been camping in the cold, and there hasn't been much stripping down and soaking lately. While she's bathing I read the information about Carson National Forest and Wheeler Peak. We picked up a bunch of brochures right at the desk of our motel.

"This is interesting, Chlo," I say, loud enough that she can hear me in the tub. "There's all kinds of stuff in here that I wouldn't have thought of on my own."

"Like what?"

"Like I was thinking if we didn't want to carry water, we could just eat snow. I mean, that's water. But it says here that it's a bad idea to eat snow. Melted snow is okay but you have to have some way to melt it. It says if you eat snow, it doesn't provide that much water. Only about ten to twenty percent. I'm not sure what that means. Maybe it means it melts down to a lot less than you think. And also it brings down your body temperature too much."

"So we'll carry some."

"I guess."

"What else does it say?"

"Well, it has a bunch of stuff about hypothermia."

"I don't know what that is."

"It's when you get so cold it kills you. It has all this stuff about preventing it. It says that cotton next to the skin keeps the body damp but wool can get wet and still provide insulation."

"Must be why Randy gave us wool socks."

"Must be."

She comes out after a time in her nightshirt and tucks into bed with me. It's nice to be warm for a change. It's nice to be in a warm bed and not have to bundle up and to be able to change clothes without freezing. We needed this break. It was a big extravagance, staying in a motel for the night. But we needed it, and I guess I feel like we earned it.

Chloe has her head on my shoulder. "We should bike up to the Taos Ski Valley tomorrow," she says.

"Why not wait a day or two? Get our strength back from biking up the mountain."

"My strength is fine," she says. "I feel fine."

"The longer we stay here, the more we get used to the altitude."

"We've been climbing this mountain for days. We've been getting used to it all this time. I want to climb Randy's mountain. We'll have to buy a camera."

"I'll go out in the morning and get bottled water and snacks that aren't too heavy to carry. And I'll get one of those disposable cameras."

We lie there quietly for a while, just thinking. I must be really tired, because I close my eyes and when I open them again, it's light. It's morning. And we're in the mountains in a town called Angel Fire. She rolls over and hugs me good morning.

"Go buy that stuff," she says. "I'm all ready to climb a mountain."

We wake up the following morning in our tent, a few hundred yards from the trailhead. We're fully dressed, each in our separate bags, wearing our ski masks and two pairs of Randy's wool socks each. The bottled water is zipped into the sleeping bags with us, because we were afraid it would freeze. Because I read in the brochure that the local lakes—Williams, and Horseshoe, and Lost Lake—have no fish because they freeze solid in the winter. And we don't want that to happen to our water.

I pull on my boots and step out of the tent, and it's still nearly dark. Nearly, but not quite. I breathe. The air is thin up here and yet there's something superior about it. Maybe that was the problem with the air in the city. Maybe it was too damn thick.

Chloe comes out to stand with me, and she has her boots on, and a look in her eyes that tells me she's ready to go. I have misgivings about climbing a mountain in the snow. But then, part of the purpose of this trip is to help leave misgivings behind. Even if we can't make the climb. What good were the advance misgivings? How did I improve things with my worry? I take a big deep breath of cold mountain air and throw them away. I won't say throw them to the wind because fortunately there is no wind. But when I breathe out again they seem to be gone.

I load up the backpack with snacks. Chocolate and string cheese and trail mix and dried fruit. And the disposable camera I bought. We zip most of the bottled water into our jackets to keep it warm. I tie the snowshoes to one strap of the pack, Randy's sign to the other. I eat a double handful of trail mix. Hold some out for Chloe and she takes a small handful. But it's so hard for her to eat when she's excited. She works off a whole different source of energy.

Then we hit the trailhead and climb.

We still haven't said a word to each other, or needed to.

The sun gradually comes out to meet us. Gradually shows us where we really are. A kind of slow surprise. It takes us about an hour or an hour and a half to reach the first stopping point, which, according to my little trail map, is Bull-of-the-Woods pasture. I don't wear a watch, though. I haven't worn one in as long as I can remember. So I'm guessing about the time.

So far it's pretty easy going, though according to the brochure we're now at about 10,800 feet. We've hit a lot of patches of snow, but I haven't been able to bring myself to break out the snowshoes yet, and fortunately we've just barely managed to squeak by without them. The surface of the snow is frozen hard from the cold night temperatures, so we can take two or three gentle steps on it before breaking through, sometimes to our waists. But it worries me a little, using snowshoes. Especially since I've never used them before.

There are two tents set up in the Bull-of-the-Woods pasture. People who, I suppose, climbed this far and then camped before going farther. But they're either back on the trail now or still asleep, because nothing and no one stirs up here.

We drink a little water. I eat some dried fruit and another handful of trail mix. Chloe makes a face and shakes her head. Then she looks at my face and whatever she sees there convinces her. She rummages around in the pack and finds a chocolate bar, and eats two squares. Eats them like they were medicine.

Then we climb on. We still haven't broken the silence of this morning.

The sun is more or less up now, the sky a faded white-blue. We climb through the forest for what seems like a long time. The altitude is becoming more of a problem. For me. Chloe seems to be doing fine. I haven't thought of it for years, but when I was a kid, my dad took us to the mountains and it made me throw up. Altitude sickness, which I haven't heard mentioned since. But I remember it was one more in a long string of demerits I earned on my father's list. One more incident he could file away to prove I wasn't him.

I'm breathing harder now, and my head is pounding, and my heart is pounding, and I pray I'm not about to throw up. After a steep mile of trying not to think about it, I drop to my knees in the snow, thinking it's inevitable. Prepared to hurl my trail snacks into the perfect, untouched whiteness. Chloe gets down on her knees beside me and holds my forehead the way I always used to do for her. But nothing happens. My stomach steadies, and nothing happens, except for my knees getting wet and cold.

"Poor Jordy," she says. Breaks the stillness for the first time today. We hold still and listen to the words, the voice, settle into the air, slightly changing the mountain atmosphere.

"It's okay," I say. "I'll be fine."

I stumble to my feet and we walk on.

After a while, the trail drops, which I was not prepared for. Drops nearly five hundred feet into an open basin. It's heartbreaking, because when we cross that basin we just have to ascend the five hundred feet again on the other side. On the other hand, it feels good to pick our way downhill for a change. It's a break I needed.

When we drop down into the basin, I step out onto the snowpack and punch through to my chest. I'm standing in snow literally up to my chest.

Chloe laughs. "Must be why Randy gave us snowshoes."

"Must be," I say.

I wrestle and climb my way back out again, and we strap on the snowshoes and step out tentatively and just stand there looking at each other. I think we're both expecting to fall through, but of course we don't. It's not nearly as bad as I thought. What did I think? I can't remember. Then Chloe takes a step. Then I take a step. It's weird. They're weird steps because you have to keep your feet so far apart. Chloe takes about three more test steps, then laughs out loud and takes off running. Well, maybe running is the wrong word. It's more of a wild, awkward dance, a spraddle-legged waddle. I'm infected by her joy, so I try it, too, but after ten paces or so the lack of oxygen gets me. I clump slowly along, watching Chloe dance and then stop and wait for me to catch up. Then dance. Then stop and wait for me to catch up.

At the far side of the basin she breaks the still again. She says, "Even if this was the only thing I ever did in my whole life, it would be worth having a life just to do this."

We zigzag up a series of switchbacks to reach the summit. Marmots scurry back and forth across the trail, and when we stop for a snack, they come close, begging for a handout. Our only real clue, so far, that this road has been traveled by many others. Of course, I only know they're marmots because the brochure tells me so. I might have called them groundhogs or prairie dogs, but based on the list of mammals we might expect to see, this has got to be them. Now, weirdly, the brochure said marmots hibernate in the winter. But it also said that if you feed wild animals, they stop acting naturally. Maybe you don't hibernate when there are trail snacks to be gained. Or maybe we're just not that deep into winter. Chloe throws them bits of trail mix to avoid eating it herself, and they plow through the snow to claim it.

By the time we reach what I think is the summit, I confess I'm in bad shape. We've been walking this ridge for what seems like hours. I feel like I can't breathe. I'm stopping to rest every few minutes. My feet ache and my hips ache. The sun is nearly overhead. I think if I have to walk one more yard, I'll just fall over and die. Or wish I could.

Then we reach the plaque mounted on the peak and it announces that we are actually on Mount Walter. Named for a guy named H. D. Walter, who loved these mountains. Just for a split second I find myself wondering why anybody would.

"There's the summit up there," Chloe says.

And she's right of course. This is a kind of false summit, about twenty feet lower and half a mile short of the real thing. I sit down hard on the rocky ground, fortunately free of snow.

"Want me to go on ahead and put the sign up?" she asks.

"I have to take pictures of you doing it," I say, barely able to breathe enough to say it.

"Oh, yeah."

"If this is so close to heaven, how come there's hardly any air?"

"Well, the closer you get to heaven," Chloe says, "the less air there is, because when you get to heaven for real you don't need to breathe anymore."

I have to admit that makes sense. A strange kind of sense, but sense nonetheless.

"You know," she says, "you're getting really good at finding beautiful things."

"Did I find this?"

"Sure. It was your idea to sell the truck and hitchhike. So you got us to Randy. So you got us here."

"I think I'm glad," I say, because I still can't really breathe.

"You know you are, Jordy. Just because there's no air doesn't mean you're not glad."

We sit for a few minutes, then walk the ridge to the real Wheeler. I push all thoughts out of my head and do it. And, you know, it's worth it. It nearly kills me, but it's worth it.

The view is spectacular, and there's something about standing on the top of a mountain you personally climbed at great sacrifice. It means something. The sky is brilliant blue. In every direction we see snowy mountain after snowy mountain after snowy mountain.

Chloe stands with her eyes closed, her head thrown back, as if having a silent conversation with heaven. "Randy is happy," she says.

"Good."

"You can't point to this joy, Jordy. You'd have to point everywhere at once. And if you point everywhere at once, then you're not really pointing anywhere at all."

I look around, breathe, close my eyes. See Randy's face and experience this briefly for him. Then I look around at the view again. And I realize that for all the joy we've seen so far, I've allowed it all to remain outside of me. It's always been over there. Look, over there. Some joy just went by. A little more just flew by. And when I realize that, I let it into me. And I *become* the joy. Just for a split second, I think I do.

Chloe says, "What's that thing?"

She's pointing to a heavy metal cylinder shaped like a miniature cannon. It's on the stone under the Wheeler Peak plaque. I open it and find it's a registry. A guest book of sorts.

"It's a thing that lets you sign your name so everybody knows you were here."

"Oh, good," she says. "Do that, Jordy, okay?"

So I write the date, and then the names in our party.

I write, "Chloe, Jordy the Cellar King, and Randy Banyan were here, with joy."

I take a picture of Chloe holding the sign and she takes one of me holding it. Then I stamp it into the ground with the heel of my boot, and Chloe takes pictures while I do. It's hard because the ground is frozen. But the stake is sharp, because Randy knew the ground would be frozen. It goes in because Randy designed it to.

"I wish we could have a picture of us on the mountain," Chloe says. "That would be a good thing to have. Not that I won't remember this anyway. But still, it would be nice."

I'm thinking of maybe holding the camera at arm's length and taking a chance on what we'd get. Just as I'm about to try it, we see the first people we've seen since yesterday. Two young guys. They're just there suddenly, sharing the peak with us, out of nowhere. There was nobody on the trail behind us, I know there wasn't. One of them shouts triumphantly and throws his hands in the air and leaves them there a long time.

The other says, "Hey. Take a picture of me and my brother?"

"If you'll return the favor," I say.

"You bet, man. No problem."

159

"Where did you guys come from? We didn't see you on the trail."

"Oh, we took the other trail. The one that comes up from Williams Lake. It's steep, man. Two thousand feet nearly straight up. Scree slopes all the way. It was great. We haven't seen anybody else all morning, till we saw you guys. You see anybody?"

"No," I say.

"Yes," Chloe says. When I look at her questioningly she says, "We saw those marmots."

"Oh. I wasn't counting the marmots."

"How can you not count the marmots?" Chloe says.

The following morning we're back in our base camp. I lie awake a long time thinking Chloe will wake up. But she doesn't, and I need to pee.

I unzip my bag and struggle into my boots and out of the tent, realizing with each step of the way how much pain I'm in. How stiff I am. My hips ache and feel tight, and there's a saddle of muscles between them that feels like it's contracted and then locked into place. I try to stretch a little, but it's no real use. It's just going to be a tough day. There are a few other tents within sight, so I have to walk a good ways to find a private spot to pee.

When I get back, Chloe is still sleeping. I lie down behind her and bump her gently with my whole body at once. "Hey, sleepyhead. All ready to bike back to Angel Fire?"

"No," she says. "Not today. Please? I want to stay here another day."

"Are you okay? Are you tired?"

"I'm fine. I just want to be not done climbing a mountain. I don't want it to be over."

"I'm not sure we have enough food and water for that. Unless I bike out and get more."

"Could you do that, Jordy? I sure would appreciate it. And could you go out and find some firewood, too? A fire would be nice, so we could warm up a little."

When I come back to camp with food in the backpack and an armload of firewood, it's nearly noon. The sun is straight up over our heads. Chloe has been joined by two large horned animals. Something in the deer family. Based on my reading, I'd have to say they're either antelope, mule deer, or elk, but I'll be damned if I know which.

Chloe is holding out a handful of trail mix and they're trying to decide if they're willing to take it from her hand. Then their heads come up and they see me and bound away.

"I'm sorry I chased off your friends," I say.

"Wasn't your fault," she says. "It was their choice to make."

I build a small fire, and we sit on both pads and both sleeping bags and warm ourselves by it. Every hour or so I go off and find a few more sticks of deadfall to feed into the flames.

Around dusk it begins to snow, but gently. Small, light flakes. I expect them to hit the fire and sizzle, but instead the heat makes them curl away or rise again, and they evaporate in the air, as far as I can tell. Chloe tells me she's sorry she's not ready to go back.

I tell her I'm not one bit sorry, and I mean it.

We've just come through Gallup, and we're bearing down on the Grand Canyon. A couple of days will do it. Chloe is pedaling faster, like she can smell it.

Things are better than they've ever been, we're both feeling happy, it's a beautiful day, and then all of a sudden a car comes by and runs us off the road.

I don't think he does it on purpose. But he does it. Swerves over, and doesn't hit us, but forces us to plow off the road to avoid the collision. I smack up against a barbed-wire fence, which rips my jeans and part of my leg, and then I fall over the handlebars onto my hands. I look up just as I'm falling and I get a flash of the car, the driver reaching down, his head down, like he's digging for something on the passenger-side floor.

I get up and run to Chloe, who missed the fence. She landed in a place where the fence line breaks for a driveway. So she came down on asphalt, and she somehow managed to get her foot caught in the spokes of the bike. She's also holding her wrist, like she hurt it when she landed on it, and the heels of her hands are bloody.

I look up, expecting the car to stop, but it never does. The guy apparently never sees what he's done. He just drives on like nothing ever happened.

"You okay, Chlo?"

"Ow. Ow, my foot, Jordy. Help me get my foot out."

I try to free it but the bike wheel turns slightly and Chloe screams. That's when I realize her foot isn't just sore. It's injured.

Then there's a man standing behind us, and he wants to know if we're okay.

"Not really," I say. "Her foot is caught, and she's hurt."

We work together, and I hold the bike wheel so it can't turn and he grabs the spokes and bends them out so her foot slips free. It really doesn't matter what happens with the bike, anyway.

Chloe is hurt, and besides, the wheel is all bent and screwed up from the fall.

Chloe puts one arm over each of our shoulders and we carry her back to this guy's car. He's got a really nice Mercedes-Benz. He's got a cell phone. He makes calls to find out where there's a hospital. A general hospital. The kind of place that won't tell you to buzz off if you have no insurance. Meanwhile, I take the trailers apart from the bikes and load everything into this guy's trunk. It doesn't close and we don't have rope, so we just drive away with it open.

"I don't believe that guy," he says. "He never even saw what he did. He wasn't even looking at the road. People drive like idiots. People can be such assholes."

I say nothing, because I appreciate his help so much, but I was just making some headway getting Chloe to think people are mostly decent.

"Jordy is trying to show me that people are okay," Chloe says. It comes out with a long breath, kind of tight and strained, and I can tell she's in a lot of pain.

"Well, that asshole certainly didn't help," he says.

We sit in the hospital cafeteria for a long time. Chloe has a big, clunky cast on her left foot and a brace on her right wrist. I have five stitches in my right thigh and a series of bandages on the smaller cuts and tears. The bikes are locked up out front, and I can only hope that all of our stuff is still with them. That our saddlebags and trailers are still full.

Chloe is staring at a bottle of Vicodin that I know she won't take.

"I guess we'll have to rethink our travel plans," I say.

"Oh, please, Jordy. I want to see the Grand Canyon so much."

"We'll see it, Chlo, I don't mean we shouldn't go, but we obviously can't bike there now."

"Oh. Right."

"I guess I'll sell the bikes and we'll go back to hitchhiking."

"We'll have an awful lot of stuff to carry."

And Chloe will be on crutches, so *I'll* pretty much have to carry it. Maybe we can wheel one or both of those bike trailers by hand.

"Well, we'll ditch the cold-weather gear. It's almost spring and we're headed to Arizona."

"It gets cold at night in the desert. Didn't you tell me that? We might need the jackets."

"Maybe. I'm thinking the snowshoes can go."

Chloe laughs, which I know is hard for her. I can see she's in an awful lot of pain.

"Why did that guy do that, Jordy? We weren't doing anything to him."

"I don't think he did it on purpose. He just wasn't looking."

"Oh. So, *is* he an asshole?"

"I don't know, Chlo. Maybe. Maybe not. Maybe he was being careless, I don't know, but maybe everybody looks away from the road for a second. Sometime."

"That guy in the nice car said he was an asshole."

"Yeah, well, it's really easy to call somebody else an asshole."

"So you don't think he was?"

"I don't know, Chloe. I just know I wish he'd looked where he was going."

We're so devoid of plans that we spend the night in the hospital lobby. Chloe sleeps on the one and only couch and I sleep on the floor. It must look strange, but nobody tells us we can't do it. Nobody has the heart to tell us to hit the road.

The next part of the trip is pretty awkward and difficult. I don't want to leave Chloe alone while I sell the bikes, and I have no idea where or how to begin selling them. We end up just ditching them instead. We have to get rides for even the shortest distances. I have to talk a total stranger into driving us from the hospital parking lot back out to the street. I'm carrying the two big saddlebags on my shoulders and wheeling both trailers. Chloe hobbles along on crutches without benefit of pain pills. We have to hitch from the street to the highway. Walking half or three-quarters of a mile is out of the question. When we get dropped off, we just have to sit there on the shoulder of the highway, more or less immobile, until another ride comes along.

But we're only about two hundred miles from the canyon. By bike, that's a long way. By car, it's less than four hours, if we can keep getting rides. I promised Chloe I'd show her the Colorado River snaking through the Grand Canyon. And damn it, if I have to abandon our stuff and carry her across Arizona on my back, that's what I'm going to do.

We get a ride from Williams, Arizona, right to the South Rim. We don't even have to pay to get in. We ride with a guy who lives in Williams and works at the visitor center.

"Take the mule trip," he says. "Best way there is to see the canyon."

He's wearing one of those string ties that I've only seen on TV.

"But Chloe's got a big cast on her foot," I say.

"Oh," he says. Like it never occurred to him. "Oh, right. Maybe that's not such a good idea, then."

But Chloe is on it already. Chloe likes mules. She's never seen a mule, that I know of. But she just knows she would like them. "But the mules are the best way, Jordy."

"But they're for people who aren't hurt, Chlo. Who can put both feet in the stirrups."

"I'll be fine, Jordy. I want to take the mules."

We're driving up a long narrow highway with nothing but forest on either side. Just undeveloped forest as far as the eye can see.

"We'll talk about it when we get there, Chlo."

"Sorry I brought it up," the guy says.

Me too, but I don't say so, because he meant no harm and I don't want to make him feel bad. Besides, he makes it up to us by letting us leave our stuff in his office for the day. Now all I have to worry about hauling around is Chloe.

The trip from the visitor center to the South Rim requires a certain amount of walking. I pick Chloe up and carry her there piggyback.

Now that the mule idea has set up camp in her head, I have no idea how to get it to leave again. I can really understand how much a thing like that would mean to her. Especially since we can't hike. But we can't do the mules, either. It's as simple as that.

When we reach the canyon rim, I set her down. We look around. I never saw the Grand Canyon before. I was so busy thinking about showing it to Chloe, but now this feels like it's at least partly about me. The only sound I hear is the wind against my ears. I feel like I can hear it whirling around the reddish green layered rock formations that stretch out into a sort of haze of distance. It sounds like I can hear the sound of it blowing through the scrub that grows out of solid rock. How does a plant do that? And can I really hear the wind blow through it, or is that just the sound it makes on my own eardrums? I had no idea the world was so big.

Dear Dr. Reynoso. The world is bigger than I thought.

I can hear Chloe suck in a long breath. "Wow, Jordy. This is even better than I thought."

I say, "Yeah. That makes two of us."

Then there's a couple there with a little girl. I didn't hear them come up. The wind and the view were too loud, I guess. A yuppie couple in their late thirties, the kind who would drive a BMW. The girl looks about eleven and has braces on her teeth. The girl watches as I let Chloe down off my back.

We sit down on one of the benches. Chloe looks around the way she did on the mountain. Like she's looking for a place to point but slowly realizing that would have to be everywhere. Everywhere at once. I can see how she takes all that physical beauty in. Lets it become part of her. Like breathing air and eating food, and then using that to make new cells and feed the old ones. I wish I knew how to do that like she does. I think I had it for just a second, maybe on the mountain, but then I lost it again.

"It's pretty, huh?" the little girl asks.

"Beautiful," Chloe says.

"I guess you won't get to hike the canyon, huh?"

"Alexis," the mother says. "Leave the lady alone." I think Chloe makes her a little nervous.

167

"It's okay. I'm still really happy I'm here. I never saw this before. Did you?"

"We were here last year," Alexis says. "But it was crowded, and we couldn't get a mule ride, and my parents promised we could come back for the mule ride. We're going tomorrow."

"We're going to ride mules, too," Chloe says.

"Actually," I say, "I'm not sure Chloe's up to the trip."

"I'm fine," Chloe says. "He worries too much."

"I agree with *him*," the mother says. "We have friends who've done it already. It's a two-day ride and they say it's surprising how tired you are when you come back. And you can't really get out of it easily once you get into it. I'd reconsider if I were you." She's talking to Chloe like she's a child. Which most people do. But in this case, it's not in a good way. She has one hand on her daughter's shoulder and is pulling her in closer. As if to say, Stay away from the lady, Alexis. We don't know quite what's wrong with her yet.

"But, Mom," Alexis says. "She's never been to the Grand Canyon before and she really wants to do it." Alexis knows there's nothing wrong with Chloe. Nothing that matters, anyway.

"Hush, hon," her mom says.

The husband speaks up for the first time. "Take a helicopter ride," he says. "They're spectacular. And you can get short rides, just a half hour or an hour. You'd see all the views and it wouldn't take much out of you."

"Sounds expensive," I say.

"Less expensive than a two-day mule trip."

"We did that last year," Alexis says. "Because the mules were all filled up."

"Was it fun?" Chloe asks.

168

"It was awesome. It was so cool."

"I don't know, though," Chloe says. "It's not the same as riding a mule. A mule is a real animal. A mule is a lot friendlier than a helicopter."

"If you were on a mule on that narrow trail," the mother says, "and you couldn't balance with both feet in the stirrups, it could be a real disaster."

"Maybe Jordy and I could ride double."

"No. There's a two-hundred-pound weight limit," the father says. "I know because I just squeaked through. If you ride double or ride hurt, you might even be putting the mule in danger. You wouldn't want to do that, would you?"

Thank you, I think. Thank you, thank you, thank you. I shoot him a grateful look and he catches it and returns a little nod.

"Then we'll have to ride the helicopter," Chloe says.

We all look quietly at the view for a few moments. I'm thinking what this is going to cost. How much money we'll have left when it's over. But it's the canyon, and we've come all this way, and Chloe has to see it.

Then Chloe says, "Will you guys do me a favor?"

"Sure," Alexis says. "What?"

"Go on the mule ride for me, too?"

"We don't understand what you mean," the mother says.

"I do," Alexis says. "I'll ride the mule for you. What's your name?"

"Chloe."

"I know what Chloe means, Mom. I think I do. You mean have fun with everything like you were there having fun, too. Isn't that what you mean, Chloe?"

"Right, like that. Just think of me while you're riding and think how happy I'd be feeling if those were really my eyes you were looking out through. And maybe I'll be able to tell when you do. I'm not sure, but maybe."

"I can do that, Mom," Alexis says.

"I guess there's no harm in that."

"I need a picture of Chloe. Take a picture of her, Dad."

"I have a picture," Chloe says.

And she does. She carries it in her shirt pocket. Has since leaving Angel Fire. One of the two pictures of us on Wheeler Peak. Taken by the brothers who appeared out of nowhere. We made double prints of all the photos, sent one set to Randy, kept one set for ourselves. But we kept both copies of this one, because it doesn't have Randy's sign in it. So there's another packed in with our stuff. We just happen to have a spare.

"Wow," Alexis says. "You climbed a mountain. Cool. That bites that you hurt yourself."

"Alexis," the mom says.

Chloe says, "It's okay, because I have you to do this for me."

"Give me one of your hairs," Alexis says.

This time the parents don't even dare interject. They've been aced out of this exchange the way I was when Chloe and Randy made their final pact. Everyone knows, on some deep level, the conversations in which they don't belong.

Chloe pulls out one single strand of blond hair and Alexis wraps it around her finger.

Chloe says, "Want another, in case you lose it?"

"I won't lose it. When we get back to our hotel I'll tape it to the back of the picture. And then when we get to the bottom of the canyon, I'll leave it. And all the way up and down I'll look at the view for you. I bet you'll know it."

"I will," Chloe says. After they walk away, after they're long out of earshot, she says it again. "I will." She's still looking into the canyon.

We sit that way for a long time, until I think I can see how the light changes slightly and changes the colors of the stacked bands of stone. The curved formations, and the spaces between them. Even the color of the air seems to change.

There's something about Chloe's eyes. Something familiar, but for a minute I can't place it. Then I can. Randy Banyan, thinking about the mountains.

Dear Dr. Reynoso. We found what we were looking for. I hope it's enough.

When we get our cue to run out to the waiting copter, I really try to help Chloe. There's a safety procedure. I would hate it if we had to miss out on this, too. This feels like a last chance. So we run—well, hobble—together like we just want to have our arms around each other. I hope nobody will notice how much I'm holding her up, keeping her from having to put weight on her bad foot and shielding her from that invisible tail rotor, the one that the safety video warned us about. I'd hate for them to know I have to handle all that for her.

A woman takes our picture before we board. I have no idea why. Either someone will try to sell it to us later, or they want some record of who all they're searching for. One bad thought after another.

The copter holds five, but it's just us and one other woman.

One very big woman. There are three seats facing forward and she sits in the middle one. A guy has to help her get the seat belt adjusted out to the max, and I can tell it cuts into her anyway. She has to wear it underneath her enormous belly, like big men sometimes do with their pants. Chloe and I sit in the two seats across from her, facing backward. I really try not to stare. But you don't see a woman this big every day. I'm not trying to be cruel, believe me. There's just this very human tendency to stare.

Chloe says to her, "I bet you couldn't get on the mule ride either, huh?"

The woman says, "What did you say?"

"Two-hundred-pound weight limit." I squeeze Chloe's hand tightly but it's really too late. "This is better, I guess, 'cause they don't even know how much you weigh."

I sense that on the one hand this woman is tired of defending herself and on the other hand it's second nature by now. "Hell they don't, honey."

"How would they know?"

"Remember when they asked you to stand on that carpet square in front of the counter?"

"Yeah."

I can tell Chloe is waiting for more information, so I provide it myself. "That was a scale, Chlo."

"You're kidding! Who knew? Well, anyway, we all made it."

"Honey," the woman says, "you're not even a blip on their seismic radar."

Chloe has no frame of reference for that comment, so she says, "I'm glad you get to go."

The woman changes right before my eyes. Her eyes deepen. She steps out of character by taking us into her confidence. "I made a reservation for a party of three," she says. I get a sense that she's just admitted a difficult thing.

Then we put on our headphones and lift off. At first we just barely skim over the tops of the trees, but we gain altitude as we go. I watch the shadow of the copter slide across the ground, watch the dull circle above, made by the near-invisible rotor.

As we get out near the rim, the theme from *2001* starts blasting into our ears. But the pilot keeps interrupting it to tell us what we're about to see. Chloe loses patience quickly and ditches the headphones altogether, so I do, too.

Then we look down and we don't see trees. We're looking a mile down into the canyon. It feels so weird, like falling. Also, there's a strong, gusty wind and the flight is a little bumpy. I look over at Chloe to see if she looks scared or sick, but she isn't any of that. She's just silently staring, eyes wide, joy radar on full alert. I'm surprised by the complexity of the canyon from the inside. The internal walls, formations, faces. I guess I thought that as I stood on one rim, I was looking across to the jagged other side. But it's more complicated than I thought. When you get inside, it's more complex than it looks. Like everything, I guess.

I look at the woman across from us and she's looking back at me. I smile, and she changes again. Softens. She ditches her headphones, too, which I take as a vote of confidence. We're all three bonded now. We're the last chance club.

"Look, Jordy," Chloe says. "There's a river down there."

I guess she forgot that I told her there would be a river. After all, that was so long ago. Connecticut was practically another life.

"Of course there's a river, Chlo. If there wasn't a river, there wouldn't be a canyon. The river carved the canyon."

"No way."

"Really."

"No effing way, Jordy."

I look to our flying companion and she nods that it's true. "That and the wind," she says.

"How can it *do* that? It's water. And air. And that's rock. How *can* it?"

"It just has all the time in the world," the woman says. "It just takes years."

"How many years?"

"Hundreds of millions."

Chloe doesn't relate to years very well, so I don't try to explain hundreds of millions. It would just be a waste of everybody's time. But I find myself looking at it through Chloe's eyes and I'm shocked to realize that she's right. It's impossible. I try to imagine how long a river would have to rage over rock to carve away enough to barely be visible. An inch, maybe. You'd have to watch for an eternity to see even an inch of change. Then I try to multiply that by forty miles wide and a mile deep. The world has been here, making itself, doing what it does, for such an unimaginable length of time. Anybody can *say* it. Hundreds of millions of years. But now I don't just say it. I actually try to understand what it means.

Since I've had this chance to see the world with Chloe, I've been doing that. Not just looking at the world, but actually trying to understand what it means. Instead of just spouting data about the realities of the world, I'm letting it inside. Letting it define a few things about me.

Now my mind is just as boggled as hers, and, you know, it's not a bad place to be.

You could do worse than to be amazed.

After the canyon we find a campground we like, and we set up camp and stay awhile. The woman who's supposed to collect fees, Esther, won't collect anything from us. She's so outraged that some guy ran us off the road and never stopped. It's like life owes us this big debt and she's going to pay us back just a little bit of it out of her own pocket.

Esther has a cabin way in the back, and she has us in for dinner most nights. We play gin, and she teaches Chloe how to knit. She liked me right away, and I think Chloe sort of grew on her. I think I really appreciate that about Esther, because it seems like with most people it's the other way around.

She thinks we should stay until Chloe can get out of this big, clunky cast and into a lighter walking cast. It seems like pretty sound advice.

There's a stream that runs all the way down the west side of the campground, and Chloe decides she wants to catch a fish. She borrows a fishing pole from Esther, and we sit by the creek all day and catch nothing. We dig worms, thread them onto the hook at great personal sacrifice, and Chloe casts her line into the water and we wait.

While we wait, we talk about things. Things we've seen. Things we think about things we've seen. What the things will be like that we haven't seen yet, like the beach at Big Sur. Or we don't talk at all. There's just the sound of running water, and birds. Now and again the faraway voice of another camper. The trees over our heads shift in the wind, so the dapple of sun and shade moves across us while we're not saying anything.

That's nice, too.

The second day we go out and also don't catch a fish.

By the third day I'm ready to do something different, but Chloe is determined to catch something. She's set her mind's eye on it, and she's not about to let go. We sit out all day and she catches nothing.

Late in the fourth day we actually get a nibble. Chloe suddenly isn't sure what to do, so I remind her how that reel thing works, and she reels it in. It's a fish, all right. It's bright and silvery, about seven or eight inches long. It flips its body desperately back and forth, swinging the line wildly. Chloe isn't sure about grabbing it. So I grab it and hold it for her. Then she holds it.

Then she says, "I feel bad for it, Jordy. That must suck to get caught. I feel bad now that I caught it."

"You want to throw it back?"

"Yeah. Take the hook out, Jordy. I want to let it go."

I free the hook as gently as I can, and Chloe flips him back into the stream. As he flies, she says, "Goodbye," and then, "sorry."

I guess it was something to do for four days at least.

When the time comes for Chloe to get a light walking cast, Esther drives us in to the hospital. Even though it's two and a half hours away by car.

She says she's going to miss us when we move on. I believe her. It must be hard to be Esther, meeting all these people who are just about to get up and go somewhere else.

We're on Route 87, headed south, between Second Mesa and Winslow. We're riding in a Volvo station wagon with a nice young woman named Dana. She's on a three-day vacation from her kids, and she's being nice to us. She wasn't planning on swinging so far east, but she wants Chloe to see the Painted Desert as much as Chloe wants to see it. Also, I don't think she's in much of a hurry to get back to her kids. She pulls off to the side of the road so Chloe and I can step out and get a better look. Breathe it all in.

It's nearly dusk, with the light on a long slant, making this world even redder and more dramatic. It hardly looks real. In front of us is a hill, stained in horizontal stripes. Tan and ocher and deep red and an almost purplish hue. The road, deep black with striking white lines and a yellow center divider, bends left to avoid the hill. The blue sky finishes off the painting. And white clouds, going to black and silver on their bottoms.

I feel like I could look forever.

"It really is painted," Chloe says.

"Well, not really painted," I say. "It's different kinds of rock, and it's stained by things like carbon and iron oxide." Wow. I actually remembered something from school. More amazing yet, I actually had some use for something I learned in school.

"Well, maybe that's how God paints," she says.

"Apparently so."

"I thought it was just the Grand Canyon," she says.

I have no idea what that means.

"You thought what was just the Grand Canyon?"

"It was *supposed* to be so beautiful. I was expecting that. But then there were all those other places on the way. And then the Grand Canyon was enough, but now here it is again. All this beauty. How many places are there? That are this beautiful?"

"More than you can count, I guess. An infinite number."

Then she throws her arms around me, which I was not set to expect.

"It's such a beautiful world, Jordy. I didn't know. I didn't know it was such a beautiful world. I mean, how could I know?"

Dear Dr. Reynoso. I think we can all breathe now. I think it's enough.

I could answer a lot of different ways, but I choose the simplest and most honest route.

"I'm a little surprised myself," I say.

"What if I'd lived my whole life and never known? Do people live their whole lives and never know?"

"Lots of people," I say. "Lots of people live in one city all their lives. Lots of other people see all the things we've seen and still don't know it's a beautiful world."

"How sad."

"Yes," I say. "It is."

"But it didn't work out that way for us." Just as I'm thinking I have Chloe to thank for that, she says, "Thank you for that."

It works both ways, I suppose. Without me she wouldn't have seen all this. Without her, I might have seen all this and still not known what a beautiful world it is. The saddest fate of all.

SIX

JINGLE BELLS

We've just made our way down from the mountains, through Flagstaff, out onto flat desert. Through Phoenix more or less without stopping. We don't like cities anymore. Chloe and I have no use for cities. But now we're hitching out in the desert alone, and it's getting late, and I'm thinking maybe we should have stayed over in Phoenix.

Chloe is clumping along on the side of the highway with her walking cast. No crutches. We're each towing a bike trailer. There's a moon out, and it illuminates the cactus just enough to make them look eerie, like arms reaching for us in the dark. But I guess if they're a bunch of cactus, they're cacti, aren't they?

We're getting a car every minute or two, but so far no one will pick us up. People like to pick you up in the daylight. Get a good look at you first.

A car pulls over and stops.

Before I even get a chance to look inside, Chloe says, "I don't want to go with them, Jordy."

I look inside. Outwardly, there doesn't seem much wrong with them. I mean, as far as I can see. It's just three guys, college age, in a big old boat of a Ford. Relatively clean-cut and all. Probably I would have jumped into their car in a heartbeat. Never thought twice. I'm still not sure why Chloe said what she said. But then the guy in the shotgun seat rolls down the window and leans out and I can tell that he's sloshed.

All three of the guys have open beer bottles in their hands or between their legs. So I guess I just have to go with Chloe's gut. Only, how do you tell someone you don't want a ride when you just stuck your thumb out and asked for one? Maybe if they're sloshed enough, it won't even matter. Maybe whatever I say will make sense.

"You know what?" I say. "Never mind. It's a beautiful night. We just decided we're enjoying walking."

"No, get in," he says. "Really. Get in. It's fine."

"No thanks, man. Thanks anyway."

"Come on, really. Get in."

"No, we're just going to go our way, okay? We'll see you."

I start walking, and I signal Chloe to walk. She's about five steps ahead of me, and she takes the signal and we walk.

The car cruises along at about three miles an hour, keeping pace.

"What'sa matter?" the guy keeps saying. "What'sa matter?" He's really drunk. Too much of his body is hanging out the window. The guy in the backseat is taking hits off a pipe. "What'sa matter? Come on. Get in. We won't hurt ya."

I decide to walk closer to Chloe. I don't want her up there by herself. So I catch up, and I go around her bike trailer on the right. My mistake. I should have gotten between her and the car. I know that immediately. But with the trailers behind us and the car beside us, it's hard to correct it now. I'm beginning to seriously wish another car would come by. So far it's just these three drunks, me and Chloe, and the spooky cacti and their shadows.

The shotgun-seat idiot leans out and grabs Chloe's ass. All three drunken fools whoop wildly at the same time. Chloe drops her bike trailer in surprise and that gives me my opening.

I drop back and turn and smash the guy in the face.

It's a great shot. Man, I swear I didn't know I had that good a shot in me. First of all, he's all drunken limp like a rag doll. Second of all, I hit him square in the nose. Third of all, it snaps his head back and he smacks it hard on the top of the door frame. One, two, three, you're out. He falls slack, hanging halfway out the window, blood from his nose running onto the road.

The other two guys get out.

"Run, Chlo," I say. "Run. Now. Get the hell away."

After each beat of words I expect her to move but she doesn't. Whether she's just a deer in the headlights or refuses to leave me alone in this, I don't know. There's not time to know.

The driver swings his beer bottle and catches me clean in the left temple, and I go down. I can feel the beer foaming as it soaks into my shirt. I can taste beer and blood at the corner of my mouth.

Everything that happens after that is only half clear.

I remember being picked up from behind and held with my arms behind my back. Two or three more solid blows to the face. With a fist this time. A fist with a ring. I clearly remember the ring. I remember Chloe jumping the guy who was holding me. I know it was her, even though I didn't see it. I know because when she hit his back she let out this exhalation of air, and a sort of accompanying sound. And in that sound I recognized her. Her voice. I think she had him by the throat because I heard some strangled sounds that weren't her. Then I think we all three went over backward. Chloe, the guy holding me, me. I landed on him, knocked the wind out of him. I remember hoping we wouldn't land on Chloe. It didn't feel like we did.

Then there was the boot. This big boot in my gut. That one last good shot. I might've rolled over and vomited, or maybe I rolled over and thought about it or thought maybe I would.

Then there were car lights, and the sound of an engine. A car door slamming. Another car door slamming. Nobody holding or hitting. A screech of tires. I wanted to look to see if they were gone for real but there was too much blood in my left eye, and somehow I couldn't bring myself to open either one.

That's really all I remember.

I come back to consciousness saying the word "ow."

Stitches are being applied strangely close to the outside of my left eye. I can feel the tug of the suture, but it doesn't really hurt. It's a deadened part of me. Still, the "ow" was appropriate. Just for other, more general reasons.

I open my right eye. There's a doctor standing over me. A male doctor. A very good-looking male doctor. I can't believe I just thought that. How could I have thought that at a time like this? I must be delirious. I must be trying to go somewhere else in my brain.

The doctor says, "Now you'll have a new scar to go with this other one."

"Great," I say. "A set."

"You must be quite the scrapper."

"No, sir. Not at all. I really try not to piss people off. It never seems to work, though."

"One more, for good measure," he says. I think he means another stitch. I hope so. I hope he doesn't mean another beating. I really couldn't take another beating.

"Where's the girl who came in with me?" I ask.

"I don't know."

"Is she okay?"

"She didn't seem to have a scratch on her, except for that cast. I'm guessing you already knew about the cast. I don't know where she is, though."

"Did they tell her she couldn't be in here?" I'm getting a knot in my stomach. The only reason I can think of for Chloe to not be in here with me is if they told her she had to leave.

"I don't think so," he says. "She was just here and then she was gone."

I have to go find her, I think.

"I have to go find her," I say.

"No, you have to lie still for a while. You have a concussion. You're under observation for a concussion. You're not going to jump up right now."

"No, I have to go find her."

"Someone else can go find her if it's that important."

"It is."

"Okay. I'll get someone to go find her. You just stay here and lie still."

He's gone for a long time. More than fifteen minutes. There's a clock mounted on the wall at the end of the room. The curtain is only drawn closed on my left. I have an unrestricted view of the clock. It's been more than fifteen minutes. Every minute or two a nurse looks around the curtain at me. What she's looking for me to do or not do, I don't know.

Then she's called out of the room for something that sounds urgent.

Another ten minutes go by. I don't appear to be under observation anymore. I get up.

I'm not saying it's an easy or comfortable thing to do. I'm just saying I do it. Slowly. Thinking I'll pass out with every move. But I steady myself against stationary things, and I don't pass out.

I look out into the hall. Several hospital employees are clustered around an open doorway. My handsome doctor is not one of them. The nurse who was checking on me is.

I go closer. So far they haven't noticed me.

"She just went crazy, I guess." One of them says that. A woman in hospital whites. "She was banging her head on the wall, and then on the mirror."

I have one hand on the wall to steady myself, and I take three or four fast strides down the hall to see.

That's when the nurse looks up and says, "Hey. What are you doing up?"

I keep striding. Just before two of them grab me by the arms and march me back to my horizontal state, I manage to get a quick look inside. It's a restroom. A single bathroom. On the wall over the sink is a shattered mirror. Shards of silver lie in the sink and on the floor. Most have blood on them. The sink has blood on it. The floor has blood on it. On the shattered mirror itself, a few blond hairs.

Dear Dr. Reynoso. All is lost.

* * *

They don't let me go in and see her until the next day.

She has bandages on her forehead and on the palms of both hands. She's barely awake. Her arms are strapped down to her sides, and at first I don't know why. And it pisses me off. Then I see that she has an IV dripping into her left hand, and that explains it. No way that needle goes in or stays in without full restraints. It still pisses me off. But I don't see that I can do anything about it. She looks alarmed to see me. That's when I realize that I haven't seen myself yet. I have no idea what I look like.

I sit down by her bed and she looks down at the sheets.

After a while she says, "Sorry, Jordy. I'm sorry I broke my promise."

"Well, you didn't, really. You just got scared."

"But I hurt myself. I promised you I wouldn't hurt myself."

"It's okay, Chlo. We're both okay."

Then we don't talk for a minute. We don't meet each other's eyes.

"I thought you would die," she says.

"It wasn't that bad, Chloe. It wasn't bad enough to kill me."

"One time I saw somebody get hit in the head that hard, and he died."

"Oh. You know, sooner or later you're going to have to tell me about all those times before you met me."

"Okay, Jordy. How about later? Can I do it later? Right now I'm just really tired."

"Okay. I'll leave you alone to rest."

"No, could you just stay with me? Could you sit here for a while?"

185

I'm discharged, so I guess I can sit any damn place I want. There are five other beds in Chloe's room. They're empty except for a thin, ancient man who's unconscious or asleep.

"I'm sorry I broke my promise," she says.

I sit with her until she falls asleep. Apparently she's on a good deal of painkillers or sedatives or both. It isn't hard for her to drift right back to sleep.

While she sleeps I get up and go into the bathroom off her room, or ward, or whatever you call it. I flip on the light and look at myself in the mirror.

I'm alarmed, too.

My left eye is swollen shut. Which of course I knew. I knew it didn't open. And I've been touching it gently, so I knew how swollen it was. But I somehow was not prepared for the full visual effect. My lip is swollen on one side, and I have a bandage covering the stitches at my temple. The side of my face is a sort of bright fuchsia, which I'm sure will be a lovely, sickly yellow-green in just a few days. It's kind of horrible.

But then I think, you know what? It'll heal. I look at the old scar on my forehead, and it's just that. A scar.

Nobody said we would get out unscarred, I guess.

Nobody said it was a beautiful world with no scars.

I make the call from the hospital lobby. Collect. I still know the number by heart. I know it's late in the evening there. After nine, anyway. But I feel like I have to do this now, otherwise the mood might pass and then maybe I never will.

I hear my mother say hello.

Then the operator says she has a collect call from Jordan and asks if my mother will accept the charges. There's a long, nerve-jangling pause. I'm thinking maybe she won't. Part of me would like that. Part of me would hate it, but I'd still be relieved.

Then she says, "Yes, operator. Yes, I will."

"Hi, Mom."

"Jordan, look. I'm sorry. I'm sorry, hon, but I can't help you. Your dad was furious that I gave you money last time. Now I need his signature on every check I write."

"I didn't call to ask for money, Mom. Could you just be quiet for a minute? I'm sorry. That sounded rude. I just need you to listen for a minute. I have something I need to say."

There's a gift shop in the lobby, where a nice, plump, middle-aged woman sells balloons and teddy bears and flowers. She's closing up for the night, and she waves at me. And I wave back. She knows me. Everyone here knows me. It's become a source of comfort.

"Mom. I just called to tell you that I forgive you. And Dad. I know that sounds weird. Me forgiving Dad. But I do. I forgive him for almost killing me and I forgive you for letting him. For pretending nothing bad happened."

"Jordan, I—"

"Just listen, Mom. Could you please just listen?"

The gift shop lady is walking through the lobby to the front door now, her heels clicking on the linoleum floor. She touches me briefly on the shoulder on her way by. " 'Night, Jordan."

"Good night, Mona."

"What did you say, Jordan?" my mother asks.

"Nothing. I was talking to someone else."

"Are you all right, Jordan? You sound like you're not all right." She seems irritated. Impatient. Like if I could just be all right, we could get this damned thing over with.

"I'm fine, Mom."

"Are you still with that odd girl?"

"Yeah, Mom. But she's . . . sick. Chloe's sick."

"I'm sorry, Jordan. But she'll get better. Right?"

"Sure, Mom. Right. I'm sure she will."

"Tell her I said hello."

"Will do."

"Was that all?"

I squeeze my eyes shut. Sigh.

"I don't think you'll probably understand what I'm about to tell you, Mom, but listen anyway, okay? Let me just say it. For me. When I was in New York, something really bad happened. I never told this to anybody before. Except Chloe. Well, she was there." And Dr. Reynoso, but . . . Keep your thoughts straight, I tell myself. Don't get off track. There's a high window in the hospital lobby, and I look up through it and see the first stars. The sky is still halfway light, but the stars are beginning to show. The desert is good for stars. "I did something bad there. I didn't mean to. On the one hand, it was an accident and I didn't mean to. But on the other hand, it really was my fault. I don't think I'm a bad person, but I definitely did this thing, and it was a really bad thing. I've been trying not to think about it since then. But then tonight I was sitting in this hospital in Phoenix watching Chloe sleep, and I thought, maybe that's how it was with Dad. And I just wanted to call and say I forgive you. Both. Because if I don't . . . If I can't forgive *you*, then what am *I*? You know? Then what does that make *me*?" I listen to the silence. Look up through the windows again and get a sense that the stars are listening, too. "I won't be calling again, Mom."

"This sounds so final, Jordan. You're not suicidal, are you?"

"Oh, God no, Mom. Nothing like that. I'm feeling really strong. I feel better than I ever have. I'm just not going to call again. I'm just tying up those last loose ends and then I'm going to go ahead with life and I'm not going to touch base with home anymore."

"I thought you'd done that a long time ago."

"Yeah. So did I. Can I talk to Pammy? Just for a minute?"

"She's asleep. It's late here."

"Oh. Okay. Well, I don't want to wake her up, then. Just tell her I love her, okay?"

"I will."

"Don't forget."

"I won't forget."

"Please. It's important. When you get off the phone, just write a note that says, 'Jordy loves you' and put it on her pillow. Okay?"

"I will. I promise."

"Thanks, Mom. Because I'm not sure I ever told her."

"Well, goodbye, Jordan."

"I love you, Mom."

"Thank you, dear. That's very sweet."

"You just can't do it, can you?" A silence that I think must strain us both. "Your own son, and you just can't bring yourself to say 'I love you.' "

"You know I'm not good with these things, Jordan."

"Right. I know that, Mom. I forgive you for that, too."

Chloe is still on the six-bed ward. This took some talking, believe me. They wanted her in the psych ward for the balance of her stay. I begged and wheedled and cajoled and they took the path of least resistance and let her stay. Anything to shut me up. Anything to keep her from freaking out again. I assured them this would help.

Still only one other bed is occupied. Mrs. Juarez, an old woman dying of stomach cancer. She's still in a good mood, though. Dying of cancer doesn't make her any less sweet. We've had other roommates over the past few days. They all checked out, one way or the other. Chloe is sleeping, just as she was when I left.

I sit by Chloe's bed again. It's dark outside, and I look out the window. It's hard to look at Chloe because her arms are strapped down. I hate that. But it's the only way to keep her from ripping out the IV. She hates having a needle in the back of her hand. She hates it so much that they have to strap her hands down. And she hates being strapped down so much that they have to keep her sedated. It just keeps going around and around like that.

"You look like you've been crying."

I look up. Mrs. Juarez said that. I thought she was asleep.

"I'm okay, though."

"I know," she says. "I know you are."

Chloe wakes in the night. It's rare for her to be awake anymore. The sedatives prevent it ninety percent of the time.

I squeeze her shoulder and kiss her on the top of the head. "My mother says hi, Chlo."

"Jordy," she says. "You need to get me out of these straps. I really hate these straps."

"I'm trying, Chlo. I've been trying to talk them into letting you go without them. But every time they do, you rip out your IV."

"I don't care."

"Well, you have to, Chloe. You have to start caring."

"So, how do I get out of them?"

"You have to stop fighting everything." I'm talking quietly because it's late and I don't want to wake Mrs. Juarez. "You spend all your energy fighting the straps and the needles. If you would leave the IV in your hand, you wouldn't have to have the straps. If you could just relax, they could treat you much better. You're spending all your energy fighting the wrong things."

"How do I just relax?"

"We've been working on that the whole trip, remember?"

"We worked on how to relax and have fun. I'm not sure how to relax when nothing is fun."

"I'll help you. I'll hold your hand the whole time. All day. I'll hold your hand and we'll talk about all the places we've seen and after a while you'll forget the needle is even there."

Actually, I'll have to hold her wrist because her hands have cuts.

"Can we sing?"

"In the morning," I say. "Not now. We'd wake Mrs. Juarez."

"Mrs. Juarez is already awake," Mrs. Juarez says.

Chloe and I both look over. Then I turn on the little light over Chloe's bed.

"I'm sorry we woke you, Mrs. Juarez."

"Don't be sorry," she says. "Pretty soon I'll get to sleep a long time. Right now I hate to miss anything. Go ahead and sing."

"It won't disturb you?"

"Fighting is disturbing," Mrs. Juarez says. "Cussing is disturbing. Singing is a good thing. Maybe I could even sing along. If it's a song I know."

Chloe says, "Do you know 'Whiter Shade of Pale'?"

"Can't say as I do, but that's okay. You go ahead. I'll just listen."

Chloe raises her voice to the song. To me it sounds like she isn't raising it very high. She sings like an angel. Tonight her voice sounds thin and, well . . . pale. To me, anyway. But then I've heard her sing before, back in the more childlike days. Mrs. Juarez hasn't.

"You have a lovely singing voice, dear," Mrs. Juarez says.

Chloe stops singing between verses, just long enough to say "Thank you."

Then she starts onto the second verse and I join along. I'm not a singer. Never have been. But I told Chloe I would sing with her, so I guess I'll have to get credit for caring enough to do it. I'll have to hope it's not the talent I'm being graded on. While we're singing, I undo the straps. Then I hold both of her wrists. If she can't move her right hand, she can't tear out the IV. If she doesn't move her left hand, she's less likely to notice it's there.

We go all the way through that song twice.

Then Chloe says, "This isn't fair. We need to sing something that Mrs. Juarez knows. What songs do you know, Mrs. Juarez?"

"Hmmm," Mrs. Juarez says.

I hold Chloe's wrists even more tightly because we're not singing. She's doing her part, though. She's trying. She's looking out the window at stars, and smiling. She really wants to get out of those straps. Even if she has to relax to do it.

"How about, 'Do You Know the Way to San Jose?'" Mrs. Juarez asks.

Chloe thinks hard, then shakes her head. "Sorry."

"What about, 'The Name Game'?"

"Is it a game or a song?" Chloe asks.

"Sort of both," she says. "You take a name. Like Chloe. And then you sing it, like, 'Chloe, Chloe, Bo-Bohee . . .'"

"I know that one," I say. "I bet I could teach it to Chloe."

"Other than that," Mrs. Juarez says, "all I can think of is Christmas carols. Everybody always knows Christmas carols. No matter how old or young you are, or what kind of life you've had, you always know all the words to 'Jingle Bells.'"

"I know that one," Chloe says. "That's the one that goes, 'Jingle bells, jingle bells, jingle all the way.'"

We start to sing it, all three of us. It's a nice, happy, rousing song, so I guess by the third or fourth round we get pretty loud.

After a while a nurse comes in. A heavy young black woman with a disapproving face.

"What the hell is going on in here?" she asks. She turns on the overhead light.

I realize we've never seen this nurse before, which is strange, because we know all the nurses here. No one in this hospital is a stranger.

"We're singing," Chloe says.

"Well, I hear *that*. You all must be crazy. Singing Christmas carols out here in the middle of the desert in the middle of the night." But she doesn't look all that disapproving anymore. Chloe is still humming "Jingle Bells" and I guess the cheeriness of it has won the nurse over to some degree.

"Who are you?" Mrs. Juarez asks. "We've never even seen you before."

"Evelyn Reid," the nurse says. "I just transferred here from Tucson."

She moves across the room as she tells us this. Busies herself checking Chloe's IV bag.

She looks at the wall beside Chloe's bed. Taped up at Chloe's eye level is the photo of us standing on Randy's mountain. Next to that are the pictures of people riding horses on the beach. The one thing we haven't gotten around to yet. "You climbed a mountain?" she asks.

"Yep," Chloe says. "We've done just about everything. Except the horses on the beach. I rode a real horse, though. I rode a horse named Margie. Just not on the beach. We went to Niagara Falls and then rode a bike all the way to the Sangre de Cristo Mountains. Then I broke my foot. Then we went to the Grand Canyon."

The nurse looks down and sees that Chloe's hands are free of her restraints. She frowns.

"According to the chart, I'm to see that this woman's hands are strapped down at all times. It says that otherwise she'll rip out that IV."

I hold Chloe more tightly. Because she's just become a lot more likely to rip out her IV. Because Evelyn Reid just reminded her it was there. "But she's not ripping out her IV," I say. "Is she?" A silence falls, and lasts. And waits. In it, I know, rests a lot that's important. A lot that could make all the difference right now. "Chloe is learning how to relax, because if she relaxes, she won't waste all her energy fighting the straps, and she won't need so much sedative."

More heavy silence. Evelyn Reid sighs. "That's right, put my job on the line, first night I'm here. If she starts getting anything short of relaxed, you ring for me, and I mean fast."

"How can she be anything but relaxed," I say, "when we're all singing 'Jingle Bells'?"

Mrs. Juarez starts up the chorus again, and Chloe joins in. Her voice sounds stronger now. I join them. The volume comes up to a cheerful sort of rowdiness.

"Sing it with us, Evelyn," I say. "Jingle bells, jingle bells, jingle all the way . . ."

Evelyn rolls her eyes. "I think you're all out of your minds," she says.

She snaps off the overhead light on her way out the door.

After we burn out on "Jingle Bells," I teach Chloe the "Name Game" song. She picks it up right away.

"That's a really silly song," she says.

"That's the beauty of it," Mrs. Juarez says back.

When we've used up our own names we do Evelyn. It's clumsy and awkward. It works better with one or two syllables. But we're not ashamed. We really belt it out anyway.

Evelyn sticks her head through the door.

"Don't even," she says.

SEVEN

JOY

We're riding a Greyhound bus west, out toward the coast. Chloe and me.

It's night, and the lights are off in the cabin of the bus, and almost everybody is asleep. Other than us, the only passenger I think is awake is an odd, disheveled man across the aisle. He has his personal light on, and he's holding a mirror, and pulling his eyelids out away from his eyes, and examining his eyeballs in the mirror. At first I thought he had something in his eye, but he's been doing it for hours now, so it must go deeper than that.

Chloe has the window seat because she likes to watch the desert go by. There's a full moon tonight, so everything is pearly and shadowy but visible. It gives me the feeling of something stolen, something I wasn't supposed to be able to see. Some treasure not normally mine.

When Chloe speaks, it's in a whisper. Only a whisper will do with all these sleeping people around. Also, this talk I feel coming is only for us, only for each other, and if the other passengers were awake, we might not have it at all. "Jordy," she says. "The trip is almost over."

I'm thinking she's about to tell me where she landed. On "everything was going fine" or on "it all fell apart again." I want to say, Don't tell me. I don't know and I don't want to know. I want to say, Don't talk about this. But that's not fair. Sooner or later we have to. Sooner. I'm beginning to think sooner.

"I know, Chlo."

If only we could have somehow ended the trip on Randy's mountain, or at the Grand Canyon. Or even at Esther's campground. If only we hadn't been hitching in the desert at night. Why did that have to happen? Why do things like that happen? I really want to know. I'm looking past her out the window, watching cacti rush by. They seem to be reaching. Just like they reached for us that night. In the moonlight they look like giant arms, reaching. Only they can't get to us, and it isn't spooky anymore, anyway. More of a lonely reaching. Only for what, I don't know. For a long time nobody whispers anything. We just watch the cacti fly by. I'm beginning to accept that they have always been reaching and always will be. I look at the weird guy across the aisle again. He's still looking at his eyeballs. I wonder what *he's* reaching for.

Chloe still hasn't said what she's decided, and I still don't want to ask. Maybe I was wrong to think she was about to tell me. Maybe I read that in. After all, we haven't seen everything yet. We haven't seen Big Sur or ridden horses on the beach.

It really isn't fair to decide yet.

I set my head down on her shoulder, and she strokes my hair.

Pets me like I was a good dog. I try not to go to sleep because we hardly have any trip left, and I hate to miss anything.

We get off the bus at Paso Robles, hitchhike to Highway 1. Then our ride is going south, away from Big Sur, so we wait for a long time at the intersection of Highway 46 and Highway 1, hoping somebody will come along and give us a ride. Lots of cars pass, but nobody stops.

It's just green pastures here. No ocean yet. Just green hilly pastures. We've been shedding belongings all along the way. Now we're down to the two saddlebags sitting on the pavement beside us.

"Where's the ocean?" Chloe asks. "I thought Highway 1 ran right by the ocean."

"Maybe other parts of it do," I say. "Maybe just not right here."

"I thought we'd see it by now."

"Well, I don't know, Chlo. Maybe pretty soon. Hopefully pretty soon."

After a minute or two a big old Cadillac comes down the road, and I stick my thumb out, fairly desperately. He stops a few yards up the road, so we carry the bags up to his car.

"Where you young folks headed?" the driver asks. He's old, maybe eighty or more. Maybe a lot more.

I pile Chloe and myself into the backseat. Then I say, "Big Sur, sir," which sounds weird.

"Well, you're lucky then, because I'm going all the way to Monterey."

Chloe asks, "Is that farther than Big Sur?"

The driver says it is.

"When will we see the ocean?" she asks. "I never saw the ocean before."

"Soon now," he says. "Another four or five miles."

We ride in silence, and at no time does he ask what happened to Chloe's face. Or to my face. Which I silently bless him for.

When we reach a stoplight at the northern end of the next town, the driver puts on his left-turn signal. He makes a left off the highway, then a quick right onto a road called Moonstone Beach Drive, and suddenly there it is, spread out before us. All the way out to the horizon.

"Wow," Chloe says.

The driver pulls off into the dirt and parks. "Not that you won't see plenty of it on the drive. But this is your first look, so get your fill."

He lets us watch silently for a few minutes.

Then he says to Chloe, or to me, or both, "What's in Big Sur?"

"Horseback riding," Chloe says. "We're looking for things that are beautiful. We have all these things we've seen, all these beautiful things, but not horseback riding on the beach at Big Sur. We saw Niagara Falls and the Rocky Mountains and the Grand Canyon and the Painted Desert. But we still have to ride horses on the beach at Big Sur."

"Those are all big things," he says. "What about little things?"

"We saw little things. We saw cats and cows and trees. But the ocean is a big thing, and I'm sure glad we get to see it."

"Not everything about the ocean is big," he says. "You should walk down there and see. Right up there. I'm going to stop up there, at Leffingwell Landing. I'm going to eat my sandwich in the parking lot. You should walk down the steps and onto the rocks. There are tide pools in the rocks. Look very close. Then when I'm done eating you can tell me what you saw."

On the drive, the man tells us his name is Maximilian. Not Max, he says; he doesn't think it's asking too much to say it out. He parks in the little Leffingwell Landing parking lot and pulls a peanut butter and jelly sandwich out of a brown paper bag.

He points to the railed, wooden stairs in front of the Cadillac. "Go look around and tell me what you see," Maximilian says.

Chloe and I walk down the rough wooden stairs and pick our way out onto the rocks. So far I only see rocks, eroded to hold little pools of seawater, with waves splashing against the far end. When a wave hits, it throws water into the air in big individual drops that sparkle like crystals in a moving chandelier. I let Chloe lean on my shoulder because her foot is still sore.

"Look, Jordy," she says. Her voice is hopeful and excited, more than it has been for a long time.

I look where she's pointing—between the vertical rock face and the rocks under our feet. There's a crevice, and it's full of little crabs. They stare out of the dark, pincers at the ready in front of their chests, doing something that looks strangely like push-ups.

We watch them for a while, which seems to make them nervous.

Then Chloe gets down on her knees on the rocks and we look more closely at the tide pools. They're filled with all kinds of life, things you might not notice at first glance.

"Shells," Chloe says.

"More than just shells," I say. "The shell is what's left when the animal dies. These are still alive."

"Those are animals?"

Just as she asks, a cone-shaped shell skitters across the pool on crablike legs. Chloe laughs.

"And all these," I say, pointing to barnacles and colorful little cap-shaped shells clinging to the rock. "These are all live animals. Now look at this." I point to a rounded stone, different-looking from the stones around it. It looks sticky, and bits of gravel-sized stones and shell have stuck all over it, decorating it. "I bet you think that's a rock."

"It isn't?"

"Touch it."

Chloe touches it, and it contracts. Draws in and squirts water. Chloe shrieks with laughter. It's so damn good to hear.

We go back to the car. Maximilian is done with his sandwich and he's eating an apple. He's cutting it up with a penknife to eat it. I wonder if that means his teeth are not his own. He's drinking a carton of milk with a straw.

Chloe tells him about the crabs, and the shells that turned out to be alive, and the rock that turned out not to be a rock at all.

"Nothing wrong with the Grand Canyon," Maximilian says. "Nothing wrong with wanting to see the ocean. Nothing wrong with *big* beautiful things. But sometimes beauty can be some pretty close work."

As we cruise up the Big Sur coast, the road goes higher. Rises up onto cliffs over the ocean, causing the horizon to stretch out. So there's even more ocean than we realized. And it's not all one color. It's dark navy out toward the horizon, turning turquoise at a fairly distinct line closer to shore. Then foamy white against the jagged rocks. Also patches of maroon-brown kelp float on the water like big shadows.

I always assumed the ocean was blue all over. Just blue.

"You're a little late for whales," Maximilian says. "But watch anyway. Who knows? Most of them go by November through March. But I've seen stragglers. Never saw one quite this late, but that doesn't mean I never will. World is full of things I've never seen."

"How would you see one?" Chloe asks. "Don't they swim under the water?"

"Oh, they have ways of showing themselves. Sometimes you see them blow. Sometimes you see a fluke come up and then slap down on the water. Sometimes you'll get to see a whale breach. That's when they throw their whole body up out of the water and then splash down again. Now that's a sight."

"What's a fluke?" Chloe asks.

"That's their big tail fin."

"Maximilian," Chloe says, "you're so old. How come you haven't seen everything already?"

"Nobody gets to see everything," he says.

"Really?"

"Really," he says. "Nobody is that lucky. We collect all the sights we can, and it's still just the tip of the iceberg. I'm ninety years old and I've only just about scratched the surface."

When we get into Big Sur, Maximilian turns off the main road and drives us downhill to a stable. A stable with horses all saddled up and ready to go. Tied to a hitching post, waiting. Randy Banyan was right again.

"Goodbye, Maximilian," Chloe says. "Thanks for showing me the ocean."

"Oh, I doubt you could have missed it," Maximilian says. "Whether I was here or not."

The woman who rents out the horses looks about fifty, and a little angry. A little hard. Her face is weather-worn and set against whatever I might be about to say.

"We want to rent a horse," I say.

"Last trail ride doesn't go out till three and it's full."

Chloe sits down in the dirt by the barn. We have no idea where we'll stay tonight. We have very little money. Pretty much just enough for the riding and for lunch. We don't have a plan B.

"Any way we can go out on a horse alone?"

"You keep saying 'horse,' " she says. "There are two of you. And besides, we don't let people go out alone. They act like idiots. Abuse the horses."

I pull her aside, off where Chloe can't hear. "The two of us together don't weigh much more than one big guy." I'm wondering if she'll charge us for two people if she only rents out one horse. "And we would never abuse a horse."

She looks past me to Chloe sitting in the dirt. "What happened to her head? What happened to your eye? You two get in an accident or something?"

I'm not sure why, but I decide the truth might work on our side. I tell her, in about the ninety-second version, why we left Connecticut, what we're hoping to prove, and how important this final leg of the trip could be in the decision. I even tell her how I got beat up in the desert and about Chloe flipping out and banging her head into the mirror.

The woman looks at me for a long time, a little cold. Still sizing me up. I don't think I'm getting through. I think I might've overestimated her. Then she says, "You think I want to give one of my horses to a girl who flips out and hurts things?"

"Only herself," I say. "She'd never hurt another living thing."

"Yeah, but still. If she's that unpredictable—"

"But that's just it. Don't you see?" She looks right into me for the first time. Like she might see if she looked harder. "This is her last chance to see something better. It's like a huge important wish. How can you deny somebody like that a chance to see something better?"

"Easy. I know people. I know what they do. You can't believe what'll happen to a horse. They get kicked, run to death. Their mouths pulled at till they bleed. Like they can't even feel the pain. Like they're just there to have fun with."

"Right," I say. "Exactly. That's it."

"That's what?"

"You just described what's happened to Chloe all her life. Don't you see?"

She looks into me a minute more, but I guess she doesn't see, because she turns and walks away. Turns her back on us and walks into the barn. I turn back to Chloe. Try to think how you apologize for something like this. Try to think where we'll go and what we'll do and how we'll get back here and when we'll get on a horse, if we ever do.

"Chloe . . . ," I say.

But she's looking past me, and her face is all lit up, beaming.

I look around and see the woman come out of the barn leading a saddled horse, a big, dappled Appaloosa. She holds the reins while I lift Chloe by her waist. Hoist her up until she can throw a leg over the saddle.

"What's his name?" Chloe asks, holding tight to the saddle horn.

"Cisco," the woman says. "Now look. I want you to really respect—" She stops in midsentence. Chloe is draped over Cisco's neck, hugging him. "Never mind," she says.

I reach into my pocket and pull out the last of our money. Twenty-two dollars.

"Thank you," I say. "Really. Thank you. How much?"

The woman shakes her head. "Can't charge for a last chance to see something better. Wouldn't be right."

"Thank you," I say again. I mount the horse behind Chloe. We barely fit in the same saddle, but we manage to. It's not comfortable, but we manage. "I don't know the way to the beach."

"You don't have to," she says. "He does."

Cisco carries us through a stream, which he fords without concern. Down a long dirt path lined with trees. The wind is high, and it makes the trees creak. Some of the smaller trees lean. Now and then we have to duck our heads. I ride with one hand on the top of Chloe's head just to make sure she remembers to duck. We see a monarch butterfly that flutters between Cisco's ears before the wind takes him away again. We ride through a flat clearing with high grass blowing like wheat and bright orange poppies scattered around.

"How far to the ocean?" Chloe asks.

"I'm not sure."

"Cisco knows?"

"Yeah. Cisco knows."

When we get to the top of the bluff we see the ocean below, a sort of horseshoe-shaped cove. Big, imposing rocks sit near the shore, churning the ocean turquoise-white all around them. We can see the green mountains behind us. See the highway wind south down the coast. When I see where we were, then I understand where we are. Then I get that we're here.

Cisco picks his way down a switchback trail with pieces of railroad ties set in every few feet like steps. One steady hoof after another. We lean back in the saddle to make his job easier.

My feet are in the stirrups, and Chloe is riding with her heels on top of my toes. Balancing on my feet. It reminds me of the way fathers teach their little girls to dance.

When we get down onto the beach we steer Cisco along the edge of the water. He doesn't seem to mind. I'm holding Chloe tightly. I'm not sure why. I guess so she can't possibly go away. She's being quiet. I'm used to that, but this quiet feels different. This goes deeper.

"Want to go fast, Chlo?"

"Ask Cisco how *he* feels about it."

I drum on his sides gently with my heels and he breaks into a few beats of bumpy trot and then a smooth canter. A wave comes high up onto the beach and his hooves splash droplets up into the air, and they land on the legs of our jeans. Then I pull him up to a stop and we stand there, Cisco's hooves planted in the wet, shiny, pebbly sand at the edge of the country. The exact opposite edge of the country from everything we knew before.

"Jordy," Chloe says. Her voice is strained and quiet with

wonder. "We did it, Jordy. We made it." We look off to the horizon awhile longer while I let the truth of that simple statement fill me up. Then Chloe says, "Jordy, let me down now."

It gives me an uneasy feeling.

"Why?"

"Just let me down. Please."

I swing down off the horse and lift Chloe down. I set her gently on the sand. "What are you going to do, Chlo?"

"I'm going to go for a swim," she says. "Just like we did in Trent's swimming hole. Only this time it's the real ocean."

"But, Chloe," I say. "It's so cold."

"I know," she says. "But maybe I'll never get to swim in the ocean again."

"I'm going in with you," I say. So I can't possibly lose her.

I expect Cisco to ditch us and run back to the barn. He doesn't. He waits patiently on the sand. Shaking his mane now and again. He must think we're crazy. Probably we are.

I sit with her by the edge of the water, Cisco standing close beside us. Chloe holds his reins. We're soaking wet. We couldn't dry off before getting dressed again, so we got our clothes all wet and sandy, and now we're sitting wet in a stiff breeze, and our teeth are chattering. But damn it, we swam in the ocean. Together.

"Thank you for taking me to see everything," she says.

I open my mouth to speak, but unfortunately I'm not about to say "you're welcome." I'm about to have this out, here and now. "Chloe," I say. "I have to tell you something. I'm not letting you go. I lied about that just to get you to go on the trip, because I was so sure it would help you. Or I wanted to be sure. I lied when I said I promised. I'm breaking my promise. No matter what you decide, I'm not letting you go."

"You're breaking your promise, Jordy?"

"Yes. I am. I'm sorry."

"How can you just break a promise like that?"

"You've broken promises to me. You promised to take your pills. You promised you wouldn't hurt yourself."

"Yeah, but I didn't know I was going to. I tried to keep them. I didn't just lie."

"I'm sorry, Chlo. I just think some promises don't deserve to be kept. I just think this is one of those."

We sit quietly for a while. We watch the whitecaps roll in, set after set. Watch them hit the rocks and throw foam into the air. Chloe is rolling Cisco's reins around in her hand.

"Well, I guess that's okay," she says. "Because I really wanted to stay now anyway."

"Really?"

"Yeah, I was thinking we haven't seen everything yet, and now I don't want to miss anything."

"That's great, Chlo. That's really good." But then I say, "Well, then why were you arguing with me about it?"

"Because it's a promise," she says. "You can't just break a promise."

"Okay. Sorry, Chlo. I promise it won't happen again."

One by one, we put our wet, sandy feet in the stirrups and swing onto Cisco's back.

I rein Cisco around and he takes us up the bluff, steadily, calmly, without hesitation. We lean forward over the saddle horn to make his job easier.

Chloe says, "What did Maximilian mean about the tip of the iceberg?"

"Oh. It's just an expression. He wasn't talking about a real iceberg."

"Yeah. It didn't sound like he was."

"The way icebergs float, about ninety or ninety-five percent of them is floating under the water where you can't see. So when someone says it's only the tip of the iceberg, it means that however much you see, there's like ten times more that you don't see."

"Oh. You would think ninety years would be enough to see everything."

"Nobody can see everything. It's infinite. There's no end to it."

"Oh. That's good, I guess. That makes it really hard for anybody to get bored."

We walk on the shoulder of the highway, a nice comfortable downhill slope.

We walk through giant redwood trees, past campgrounds and rental cabins.

We walk until the ocean is stretched out at our feet again.

We can see miles down the coast. The coastline itself sits in fingers, in folds, with scatterings of rock strewn at its fingertips. We can see all the way down to a bridge with high, curved supports rising up from the water to the road.

I realize we only have twenty-two dollars to our name, but it doesn't really matter. One way or the other we're starting all over from scratch. We have twenty-two dollars in my pocket and the future is open in front of us like a calendar with no dates written in yet. It's a blank book. It can be anything we make it. It can be anything. It can start right now.

I look out toward the horizon and I think I see a spout—a chute of water—fly up into the air. Just as I'm convincing myself it's only my hopeful imagination, the fluke rises out of the ocean, then slaps down with a splash and disappears again.

Chloe sees it, too. She raises her hand and points to it, in case I don't see.

"There, Jordy," she says. "Right there."

April 14

Dear Dr. Reynoso,

Chloe and I were going to write you a letter together. One letter between us, answering your question. Telling you what we decided about the world. Then I started thinking it would be better if we did it separately. After all, we each have a brain and a pair of eyes, and even though we saw the same things, we couldn't possibly have seen them the same way or drawn the same conclusions.

I hope you even remember that you asked me to do this. I'm figuring you wouldn't have said it if you didn't really want to know. At first I thought you would write back and say if I was right or not, like a test. Now I wonder if you asked because you weren't entirely sure yourself.

Well, here goes.

We met a lot of people all over the country. We found out that people all over the country are pretty much the same. Most of them are helpful and sweet. Some of them are crazy and thoughtless and careless and mean. More of them were helpful and sweet, though. In fact, so many people went out of their way to treat us like family that it was really hard when we got run off the road and I got beaten for no particular reason.

I was thinking at first that it would've been a lot easier to believe in the beauty of things if that hadn't happened. But now I feel like anybody can think the world is beautiful when it's all going their way. That's just like untested faith. But when you've got one eye swollen shut and you still know it's better than it is bad, then you're onto something.

I hope I'm making any sense here at all.

My conclusion is this: It's a beautiful world, but also a scary one. I used to think something couldn't be both. But then I remembered the point of no return on the Niagara River, and how much it fascinated me as a kid. Because it was just that: beautiful and scary. It's like once you get that sense that there's no real security, that anything at all can happen to you, then every minute you're okay is a joy. Part of the joy is feeling like you can make your way in a world that isn't always easy.

Anyway, that's what I decided. Chloe can speak for herself.

I think she's a little bit afraid to write to you, because she thinks you'll be mad that she told me all the stuff that happened to her before we met. She thinks you'll be upset because she finally told me, but she would never tell you. I wanted to tell her that no one would be that small. I wanted that to be one of Chloe's misunderstandings about the world. But the world is full of small people. I just don't believe you're one of them. So I told her you're not like that. Don't make a liar out of me, okay?

By the way, I thought about what you said about me having a life of my own. I'd like to say I've been dating, but the truth is, it's hard to find a guy who doesn't mind getting Chloe in the package. Now I know how single mothers feel. But it's okay, and I'll tell you why. Because when I find the right guy, that's how I'll know. Chloe will be my litmus test. What do you think? I like it.

Yours sincerely,
Jordan

✻   ✻   ✻

April 14

Dear Dr. Reynoso,

Jordy says you want to know what we think about the world. I didn't know you wanted to know that. You never told me you did. Jordy says you said it while I was sleeping. But sometimes I wonder if maybe you said a lot of things that didn't quite go through to me at the time. Sorry.

Anyway, if you want to know, I'll tell you.

Jordy thinks the world is more beautiful than it is ugly. I've decided he can think that if he wants. After all, he always lets me think what I want. Here's what I think. I think the world is just as terrible as beautiful and just as beautiful as terrible. I think things can only be as good as they can be bad. Maybe I'm not saying it right.

Like rain. Take rain. It grows trees. But then you can't even sleep if you don't have a house. Or fire. It's real warm when you're in the snow, but then it burns your house down.

Now do you see what I mean?

Maybe you don't because you didn't see everything we saw. You can't believe everything we saw. I would tell you, but it would take so much writing. I'd be writing for most of the rest of my life, and while I was writing, I'd be missing more stuff.

Even though you want me to, I'm not going to say how I made up my mind. Because I haven't seen everything yet. How can I make up my mind when I haven't seen everything yet? Maximilian is ninety and he hasn't even seen the tip of the iceberg. So what I've seen is maybe not even the tip of the tip.

Maybe when I'm ninety I'll write again.

Are you mad because I told Jordy all that stuff I never told you? He says you won't be. He really likes you, you know. He trusts you. And Jordy doesn't trust just everybody. Now I wish I'd been paying better attention back then. I bet I would've trusted you, too, if I'd been paying attention. I always liked you. But now I get that I missed a chance to have somebody I could trust. Besides Jordy, I mean.

Here's why I told Jordy and not you. Because I know him better. And because I sort of felt like he earned it. I hope you understand. Do you understand?

Thanks for trying to help me even though I would

hardly talk to you or anything. That must be hard for you when people do that to you. If you didn't like me back then, that's okay. I understand. I bet you would like me now.

Oh, and guess what? I think Jordy is going to get me a dog. He doesn't think he is. But I think he is. I think I'm wearing him down.

Love,
Chloe